TRAPPER CREEK

The Last Hunt

G. A. OSBORNE

DEDICATION

In memory of my Father and Mother

PRELUDE

Sam and John are high in the mountains of Montana on a hunt for a monster bull elk and are lying in ambush, waiting for the trophy of a lifetime to come into bow range. The setup is perfect, and the massive bull is just a few yards away. Now is the time to finish the deal.

But there is also another hunt happening in the valley far below them. Four FBI agents are closing in on three heavily-armed, violent criminals dead set on making their escape.

CHAPTER 1

Bow season in Montana is only two weeks away, and the bull elk are in rut. Early morning bugles echo across the crisp mountain air. Herd bulls thrash the ground with their antlers, ripping out huge chunks of earth, preparing to defend his cows against all newcomers trying to break into his harem. Brutal battles take place as aggressive bulls spar to establish dominance over territory and harems.

Fall has come to the mountains of Montana. In the high alpine meadows, the leaves on the tall aspens have turned different shades of yellow and brown as they slowly make their way to the ground. The needles from the massive larch carpet the ground with a golden layer. It won't be long before the fall colors give way to deep layers of snow as the cold, harsh winter takes its grip.

For Sam Conner and John Turner, almost a year of planning and preparation has ended. The backcountry hunt is approaching fast.

Sam is a seasoned outdoorsman and hunter. At sixty-six, his wrinkled face shows his age. His hands are scarred and rough from years of hard work. When he was twenty-eight, he was hit by a car while riding his Harley. A twelve-inch scar from the ensuing knee surgery runs along the side of his left knee, with four additional minor surgeries to his knee over the years. Sam deals with the pain, and after so long, to him, it just seems normal.

Sam started hunting as a young boy, roving the deep southern woods alongside his father. At eight, his parents bought him a Marlin bolt action 410 shotgun. Each fall, Sam ventured out with his dad into the hardwood forest and swampy marshes of Florida to hunt gray squirrels and wild hogs in the dense stands of oak and dogwood.

After high school, Sam's parents moved their family to a small boom town in eastern Montana. His dad had taken a job with a company in the beginning stages of starting up one of its new coal-fired power plants.

Fresh out of high school, Sam started working as a laborer at one of the nearby coal mines, then later began working maintenance with the power company. For years,

Sam and his dad hunted the open sagebrush plains and thick-timbered breaks of eastern Montana for huge mule deer bucks and pronghorn antelope. In the west, they hunted elk in the rugged mountains of the Gallatin range that borders the northern portion of Yellowstone National Park.

Years later, when Sam's Dad retired and moved to the northwestern part of the state, Sam continued working at the power plants for ten more years. Then he, too, moved to the Northwest, where he went to work in the timber industry, working maintenance on the graveyard shift at the Baylor Sawmill just north of Kalispell, Montana. After twenty-three years at the mill, Sam had his sights set on retirement just five more years away. Sam worked alone on his graveyard shift after the mill shut down for the night. He repaired and maintained the mill's massive equipment before startup the following day.

Once in a while, the company would give Sam a trainee to work with him on graveyard—usually, some young person with minimal experience in maintenance, if any at all. But most of the time, they would only last a short while before graveyard shift, and its demanding work conditions would prove too much for them, and they would quit and move on.

This is how Sam met John, his newest trainee, a young man half his age who just moved to Montana from Arizona with his wife and daughter.

When John got introduced to Sam as his next trainee on graveyard shift, Sam only had two questions for him. First, he asked John, "How much do you know about maintenance or being a millwright?" Sam was expecting a line of bullshit, so he was surprised when John told him, "Not much, but I'm a hard worker and willing to learn." Impressed with his honesty, Sam asked, "How do you feel about working on graveyard?" Once again, Sam was surprised at the young man's answer. "I'm good. I was hoping to be put on graveyard." That also surprised Sam. It was rumored that Sam wasn't the easiest to work with and was known for his sometimes hardcore attitude.

John had been working on the day shift at the mill for a few months while trying to get into maintenance. He had never met Sam but had seen him every morning in the shop before Sam left after his shift.

After years of working industrial maintenance, Sam could spot a bullshitter from a mile away and didn't have much use for them. He hoped for someone with millwright experience on graveyard, but it's been proving impossible to find over the years.

John's honesty impressed Sam, and he told John what would be expected of him. In return, he would teach John everything he knew about maintenance and being a millwright if he was willing to learn.

Before moving to Arizona, John had graduated high school in a small town in Illinois. After working at a shipyard on the Mississippi River near his home, John was no stranger to hard work. The first step he took was to pick up some welding and cutting skills, which would prove helpful with his new job.

John shared the same love for the outdoors as Sam and, growing up, had hunted Whitetail deer with his dad on their small family farm. John grew up in a Christian family and relied on his faith every day. By no means a saint, he was nevertheless a good and honest man in a world where those were in short supply. Growing up, he could also hold his own in a fight when he had to. John is laid back and doesn't let much bother him or get under his skin. Almost the opposite of Sam, but for some reason, the two men hit it off.

CHAPTER 2

Two states away, on a dark stretch of Washington highway just a few miles from the Idaho border, a County Sheriff slowly followed behind three men in a suspected stolen pickup used in a string of violent, armed robberies and a successful assault on an armored cash transport in Spokane. On his radio, the Sheriff called in for backup. Sheriffs and state troopers from Idaho and Washington were responding and rushing to set up a roadblock ahead of the pursuit.

The three men in the truck were well-armed with handguns and high-capacity assault rifles. They had no intention of ever being taken into custody.

As the truck neared the roadblock, the pursuing Sheriff switched on his light bar, and a bright spotlight lit up the three men in the truck. Imminently, a high-speed chase began. The Sheriff could see one of the men on the passenger side reach out the truck's window with a rifle. Flashes from the assault rifle lit up the sky as bullets smashed into the patrol car's windshield. The sheriff swerved, trying to avoid the hail of bullets. "Shots fired, shots fired," he screamed over the radio. The sheriff backed off. Then he reached out his window with his service weapon and returned fire. Again, he yelled on the radio, "Shots fired!"

The Chevy pickup quickly approached the roadblock at speeds of ninety miles per hour.

When the truck sped around the next curve in the road, they were met with a wall of flashing lights. Suddenly, the driver of the truck smashed hard on the brakes, then slammed the truck in reverse. Smoke poured from the rear tires before slamming into the patrol car behind him. The heavy steel bumper on the truck crushed the grill of the patrol car, sending the bull bar into the radiator. The officer fired his weapon at the driver before having to duck down to avoid another hail of bullets. When the fugitives spotted a gravel road to the right that headed into thick timber, the tires on the pickup spun and smoked on the asphalt as it quickly turned toward the gravel road.

As the truck sped down the road, dust from the gravel filled the air behind them. The three men could see a trail of flashing lights through the thick dust as they sped onto the gravel road.

Determined to escape, the Chevy roared and slid around every sharp corner. Then, suddenly, the road came to an abrupt end. A heavy steel gate and a huge Kelly hump blocked their escape. After abandoning the Chevy, the men grabbed their weapons, two duffel bags full of ammo, and two large black bags of money from their robberies, then disappeared on foot into the thick timber.

The gravel road headed east into Idaho, ending close to the town of Priest River. The men stayed in the timber and were determined to cover as much ground as possible before sunrise. One of the men had grown up in the panhandle of Idaho and knew the area like the back of his hand. He told the other two men they could make it into Idaho and steal another vehicle. Then, they could escape into Montana and, after that, Canada.

A massive search was being assembled for the armed men. But, as the fugitives scrambled through the woods in the dark, they stayed close to the gravel road.

After reaching a paved road, the men hid when they saw the flashing lights of a patrol car speeding to join in the search. After it passed, the men headed towards the distant lights of a town, darting into the timber to hide each time they saw the lights of a passing car. The men laughed about how they shot up the patrol car and talked about spending their share of the money.

Not long on the road's edge, they came across a mailbox and a driveway leading to a log home. In the driveway sat a newer Dodge diesel pickup. Next to it was a black Dodge Charger.

The driver of the Chevy pickup had his eyes on the car, then spoke up and said, "Well, what do you know, that Charger will do just fine."

While he walked over to check out the car, the two other men crept onto the cabin's porch. A light was on inside; through a window, the two men saw a young couple sitting at the kitchen table with their small dog lying on the floor. Suddenly, the couple's dog heard something and barked as it ran to the front door. The young man got up from the table and went to see what was the matter. He peeked out the window, expecting to see some deer or other animal that had caused his dog to bark. Instead, he saw a man calmly standing by the Charger. He opened the front door and yelled.

"Hey, can I help you, Buddy?"

Not seeing the two men on the porch, he stepped out from the front door. Suddenly, the two men rushed across the porch, knocking him into the house and to the floor. The young woman screamed as one of the attackers grabbed her by the hair, slamming her to the floor.

Holding the couple at gunpoint, they tied them to the kitchen chairs, using power cords they'd ripped from lamps and kitchen appliances. When the third man entered, he quickly found the keys to the Dodge Charger.

After seeing the couple tied to the chairs, he said, "It's time to get the hell out of here, Now!"

"What about them?" asked the man, pointing his handgun at the young couple.

"Make sure they are tied up good and find their phones. We'll be long gone before anyone finds them."

After loading the heavy bags of ammo and the bags of money into the Charger, they piled into the car and set out for Montana.

CHAPTER 3

S am was waiting outside when John finally pulled up.

"Well, once again, we're getting a late start," Sam said, pointing at his watch when John exited his truck. John just shrugged his shoulders.

"I hear you. I'm late again, But I have a good excuse this time."

"What is it this time?" Sam said while trying to be serious.

John smiled and said, "My wife just told me she is having a baby."

"Holy crap, congratulations, buddy, that's great news." Sam looked back at his watch and, while trying to be serious again, said. "Well, you're still late!"

After years of working with Sam, John was used to his good friend giving him crap about being late. John hoped that after Sam retired, it wouldn't matter much. But it was just the opposite. Sam had all the time in the world to get packed up and ready. Even when they would go fishing, Sam would be waiting outside with the bass boat hooked up to his truck and sitting on the tailgate with a cup of coffee, pointing at his watch.

It never really bothered Sam, but he didn't let John know. He was happy to have such a good friend to hang out with that could put up with his crap. The two men have bummed around together for years. Fishing, hunting, and exploring all over Montana. Sam's retirement has done nothing to change his role as John's mentor. Even with Sam's occasional grouchiness, they've managed to remain good friends.

Years of hard work and injuries have taken their toll on Sam, with the countless surgeries on his left knee and shoulder. Now that he's retired, managing the pain is easier, but he knows he has to take it easy, which is easier said than done.

John is young and healthy, but hard work has also taken its toll on him. Still, he keeps a close eye on his old buddy and doesn't let Sam get into more than he can handle.

Sam and John got lucky in the state draw season. Both drew special elk permits for bulls in an area known to hold some world-class animals.

Both men have been practicing with their bows at home and a nearby bow range all summer from twenty to seventy yards and everything in between. Life-sized targets at the local bow range were set up along a trail that wound across a timbered hillside. At the range, they set up different scenarios at each target while taking turns at the target.

John's bow is Mathew's new flagship bow, the VX-3, and at a seventy-pound draw weight, it's capable of hurling a carbon fiber arrow tipped with a 120-grain broadhead at 336 feet per second; it's nothing short of lethal. Sam shoots a new Bowtech SR350 dialed down to a sixty-five-pound draw weight. It is also deadly. Both bows can down any North American big-game animal with a well-placed shot.

~ ~ ~

Sam had secured a remote national forest cabin as their base camp for the hunt. It was at the end of a little-known forest road called Trapper Creek. There was only one way in and out.

The Trapper Creek cabin is surrounded by miles of national forest land and nestled right next to the Cabinet Wilderness. Not far from the Idaho border. The cabin is secluded, even though it's available to rent during the summer and early fall. It's too rustic for all but the hardiest outdoorsmen.

Inside is a small wood-burning stove and an old kitchen table with two wooden chairs sitting near a stone fireplace. Two sets of bunk beds made of two-by-four lumber provide the sleeping area. A couple of old white cabinets hang on the back wall, complete with a coffee pot and one other pot for boiling water from a nearby stream.

The Trapper Creek cabin is usually empty and mainly used as a warming cabin for snowmobilers when the deep snow blankets the forest. Occasionally, a trail crew from the Forest Department will use the place in the early summer as a base camp when they are clearing the trail into the wilderness.

~ ~ ~

Sam had all his gear packed in his ninety-nine Jeep T.J. and helped John load his gear into the Jeep. "Damn, Buddy, do you think you brought enough stuff?" Sam said with a laugh.

"Well, you know me," John said. "I've got to have all my stuff, just in case." Sam shook his head and fired up the Jeep.

Sam had purchased the old Jeep as a retirement project and, with John's help, had built it into one hell of a hunting rig. Almost everything from the ground up was new and improved; a rebuilt 4.0 liter straight six sent power to the Dana 44 axles. The thirty-five-inch all-terrain tires provided the grip. It's Sam's pride and joy that he proudly named the "Jeep." Even though on the back window above the spare tire, there was a large sticker that Sam's wife had given him. It said, "The Money Pit."

The two men were heading to the hunting area to spend a couple of days scouting before the season opened. First, they planned to tent camp somewhere away from the cabin, just in case someone had it rented out. Then, they would spend two days scouting for elk and go to a mountain lake to do some fishing.

Sam liked to be prepared and had spent countless hours researching satellite and forest maps of the area. On his computer at home, he mapped out and set wave points using a GPS navigation app, then transferred it to his handheld GPS, which he would use to help navigate his and John's position during the scouting trip.

Sam hoped to cover a lot of ground during the trip and felt that he and John had done everything possible to prepare for the hunt. The only thing left was to find elk.

CHAPTER 4

Outside of Blake, Montana, a sleepy little town with a single convenience store, two gas pumps, and a small eight-room motel. Several seasonal rental cabins sit close to the river on the opposite side of the road from the motel. Blake sits in the lush valley of heavy timber and small, crystal-clear lakes nestled in the foothills of the rugged Cabinet Mountains. The town is home to only a few residents during the fall and winter. Open year-round, the rooms at the motel are occasionally occupied by hunters during the general rifle season. Then, later in the year, snowshoers and cross-country skiers take advantage of the snow-packed and well-groomed trails.

During summer, Blake comes alive with the first people arriving at their vacation and summer homes shortly after the end of the school year and during the first days of summer break. The motel is packed with adventure seekers eager to explore the great outdoors or relax next to one of the cool mountain lakes. The rental cabins are always booked right up until the end of the season.

~ ~ ~

Lying low in a run-down, abandoned house one mile south of Blake, secluded and off the grid, the fugitives plan on waiting for the pressure of the search to pass them by. Before, they hid the Charger in the small garage attached to the house. The men would need fuel for the car and food if they were to stay there long. It was a risky chance, but one of them needed to drive to the small town.

In Blake, the convenience store, has well-stocked shelves of food and supplies—everything the fugitives needed—while a sporting goods area stocked with fishing and hunting supplies is against the back wall. Two small tables sit next to the small deli, where you can enjoy freshly made sandwiches or your morning coffee.

Jack told Troy to take the car into the small town, fill it up, and pick up some food. Troy was happy to get away for a while, even if it meant playing errand boy.

~ ~ ~

Sam's Jeep is better equipped for off-road, but it purred down the highway, not fast, but good enough for Sam.

The trip to the hunting area was only three hours away from Sam's home. First, the highway climbed over one mountain pass, and then it dropped toward the valley floor. On the pass, the Jeep slowed to forty miles per hour. Jokingly, John laughed, "Is this all she's got?"

Sam just stepped harder on the gas pedal. "Yep, that's it, but on the downhill, when this thing hits fifty-five, you're going to see some serious shit!" Both men laughed as the Jeep finally reached the top of the pass and started its descent to the valley floor.

"We better stop and gas up in Blake," Sam said.

"Sounds good. I could use a drink and stretch my legs, maybe some snacks too."

When Sam pulled up to the gas pumps at the convenience store, a Dodge Charger was sitting at one of the pumps.

"Sweet," Sam said, referring to the car.

"Yeah! That's got the supercharged Hemi in it." John replied.

When John got out of the Jeep and went into the store, a man was arguing with the cashier about not being able to break a hundred-dollar bill. Hearing what was going on, John said, "Hey, I can break that hundred for you."

At the counter, the aggravated man spun around and said. "Thanks, buddy. I was about to lose it."

John gave him five twenties in exchange for the hundred-dollar bill. Then the guy turned around and slammed forty bucks on the counter. In a disgusted voice, he said, "That's for the gas, and here's a hundred for beer and shit. Keep the damn change," Then he stormed out of the store.

"Wow, what is his problem?" John asked.

The cashier looked shaken but replied, "I don't know. I've never seen him around, but he's a heck of a tipper."

When the guy started pumping gas into the Charger, Sam was still pumping gas in the Jeep. "Sweet ride," Sam commented, "I bet it's quick."

Glancing over at Sam, the driver replied. "Not damn fast enough."

After Sam finished pumping gas, he leaned against the Jeep, waiting on John when the guy finished pumping gas in the car and opened the door. Sarcastically, Sam said, "Hey, drive safe!" Then, not even looking up at Sam, he slammed the door and took off, leaving a burnout when he hit the highway.

When John came out of the store with the drinks and snacks, Sam said, "Man, the guy with the Charger was a real asshole."

"Yeah, sure was. Just some dick with a lot of money."

All fueled up, John and Sam were back on the road. "Only twenty more miles to go," Sam said.

John chuckled, "Cool beans, but then we have eight miles after we hit Trapper Creek, right?" Sam patted the dash of the Jeep, "Yep, that's when it's going to get fun."

The old road to the cabin was nothing more than a Jeep trail that climbed up long, rocky switchbacks before ending at the Trapper Creek cabin. As the Jeep bounced over rocks and washouts, John held on tight to the "Oh Shit" bar above his head.

"This is a hell of a road," John exclaimed.

"Boy, I guess that's why we're bringing my Chevy instead of your Ford when we come back." John was a Ford guy, and Sam was Chevy all the way.

Both guys have argued and made jokes about Fords and Chevys since the day they met.

With his death grip on the bar above his head, John said, "I still wish we could bring the Jeep back. This road is a bitch."

"Yeah, me too, but we'll be bringing too much gear."

The Jeep was built for these roads, but there was little room for much gear. If John or Sam were lucky enough to fill even one of their tags, getting an elk and all the gear out would be a nightmare with the Jeep.

When they finally reached the cabin, it was empty and didn't look like anyone had been there all summer.

"Heck, we might as well camp here," Sam suggested.

"Up to you, buddy." John always left things up to Sam, maybe because he was the old guy or perhaps he just figured Sam would do what he wanted too anyway.

CHAPTER 5

The two men who stayed behind were standing on the porch. When Troy pulled the Charger up to the old house, Jack Bishop, the self-proclaimed leader and so-called mastermind of the violent robberies walked off the porch and over to the car.

A hardcore criminal, he had done time in Washington state for armed robbery and drug possession. An ex-gang member and so-called survivalist, Jack is covered with tattoos, and one large Swastika is tattooed on the back of his neck. He is tough as nails and hates the government and law enforcement. While in prison, he met Hank Barnes and Troy Becker. Hank, the other man on the porch, is a hardened gang member out of Seattle who's been in and out of prison on drug charges. He had already piled up a list of arrest warrants after being released from prison and was a suspect in recent drive-by shootings in the outer Seattle area. He, too, shared Jack's hatred for authority.

Troy was out of place. In his mid-twenties, he had spent most of his life in and out of foster homes as a kid in Montana, with a long list of drug-related misdemeanors. Troy later moved to Washington, where he met Jack while in prison for simple assault after he'd lost control and punched out a bartender for refusing to keep serving him. In prison, Troy told Jack about a back road into Canada he used when hiding out on his four-wheeler from local cops. So Jack decided this would be the road they would use to escape into Canada.

When Troy got out of the car with two bags of beer and a bag full of deli sandwiches, Jack asked, "What the hell took so damn long? Did you run into anybody?"

"Not really," Troy replied.

Jack got in Troy's face. "What the hell does 'not really' mean?"

Handing one of the bags of beer to Jack, Troy said, "Just a couple of rednecks in a Jeep."

"Did you talk to them?"

"Hell no, I didn't say a damn thing."

~ ~ ~

Sam changed his mind at the cabin and decided to backtrack about half a mile to a spot they saw on the way to the cabin to set up camp. Even though he didn't believe anyone else would be showing up at the cabin, he figured it would be best. It was a level spot with plenty of room for Sam's big canvas tent. There was plenty of firewood lying around, and the tall, rugged peaks of the Cabinet Mountains provided a breathtaking view from camp that looked like something straight out of a postcard. In the distance was a high alpine meadow where they could set up the spotting scope at camp and glass later that evening before dark.

Sam and John set up their two cots and sleeping mats in the tent. When John pulled his sleeping bag out of the stuff sack, feathers and down floated to the tent's floor. Sam just shook his head.

"I thought you were going to get a new bag?"

John's old G.I. goose-down sleeping bag had seen better days. Sam laughed as John laid it on the cot, then started fluffing it up.

"You're such a dang hillbilly."

John laughed. "Yep, you got that right."

Between the two cots sat a two-burner propane heater on a small camp table. It was late August, but it could get cold in the Montana high country at night, so the small heater could come in handy.

Sam started building a fire after he and John finished setting up camp and built a rock fire pit. As usual, John got a little carried away and gathered enough firewood to last a week. Finally, the two men relaxed in camp chairs beside the fire. Sam poked at the fire with a stick, "This is the life, isn't it?"

"Sure is. I love it." John replied.

Around the campfire, the two men bullshitted about everything: family and faith, past adventures, politics, and work. Sam sometimes gave John crap when he would ramble about some conspiracy theory or something he read online.

Later that night, after Sam had cooked dinner over the fire, he walked to the Jeep and got his elk bugle. Walking away from the sound of the crackling fire, he gave out his best call. It echoed in the calm night sky. After a minute, he blasted out another, followed by several grunts. Then, suddenly, off towards the alpine meadow, a single bull ripped out a long deep, bugle.

"Holy Crap, did you hear that?" John said.

"I sure did. That's pretty damn exciting."

Shortly after that, another bull broke his silence. Excited, Sam said, "That's awesome! It sounds like the elk are definitely in the area."

"Hell yeah, this will be our year, Sam."

After letting the fire die down, the two men entered the tent. John crawled into his sleeping bag and said, "Good night, old timer." Sam reached over and shut off the lantern and said, laughing to himself.

"You too, Princess,"

The red glow from the fire shined into the tent. Soon, John was out like a light. Sam unzipped his sleeping bag and felt around on the floor for his earplugs just as the deep snoring came from John.

Sam was an early riser. Even at home, he would wake up at four a.m., have two or three cups of coffee, then head into his shop to start working on some project. Sam decided long before he retired that he wouldn't be one of those guys who retired and then sits around doing nothing. So when he didn't have some project in the shop or around the house, he would get up early and throw his fishing gear in his bass boat and be the first one on the river, or else he'd load up the Jeep and take off fly fishing the remote rivers and lakes. Sam loves the outdoors of northwest Montana. In the Jeep, he's explored almost every forest and logging road from the Clark Fork River to the Canadian border.

Last summer, Sam invited John to go with him and his son on a three-day float trip on the lower Flathead River.

The Flathead River is a wild, scenic river. From the Canadian Rockies in British Columbia, the North Fork flows south as it winds along the western border of Glacier National Park before meeting up with the Middle Fork which makes up Glacier Park's eastern border with its headwaters in the Bob Marshall and Great Bear Wilderness of Montana.

Meeting at the Middle and North Fork confluence, the South Fork makes its way from the Bob Marshall and through the Hungry Horse Dam. All three forks make up the Flathead River that pours into Flathead Lake.

At the southern end of the lake is Kerr Dam. The section of river below Kerr Dam, commonly called the Lower Flathead, is a big river with a vastly changing flow controlled by the top spill dam. The water is warm, unlike the upper portions. Two miles below the dam, the river drops into a narrow canyon. Large rocks and roller coaster waves comprise the class three and four Buffalo rapids with the famed fourteen-foot drop that gives the rapids their name. Buffalo rapid stretches halfway across the river, and only the most experienced whitewater rafters and kayakers attempt the huge rapid during high flow. After the rapids, the river slows dramatically and begins its calm, slow seventy-mile journey, passing under Buffalo Bridge, the 'take-out' for the adventure-seeking whitewater rafters and kayakers. Buffalo Bridge is also the 'put-in' for floaters seeking to avoid the most challenging rapids. It is also where anglers begin their float through open grasslands and tall bluffs. The warm water is home to thousands of smallmouth bass and the ever-hungry northern pike.

John was new to fly fishing and only took it up after being pressured for years by Sam. So, the three-day float trip would be John's crash course in the art.

Quickly picking up the technique, John started landing smallmouth after smallmouth. Over three days, the constant shout of "Fish on!" could be heard from the three men.

By the time they reached the take-out on the third day, at the confluence of the Clark Fork River, the three of them had caught and released a hundred-sixty-eight smallmouth bass and eight large pike, and, surprisingly, Sam's son had even caught one beautiful rainbow trout.

CHAPTER 6

S am quickly started a roaring fire early the next morning. Overnight, the clear sky had allowed the air to cool and the temperature to drop. A slight breeze helped to chill the air. After sitting by the fire and finishing his first cup of coffee, the smell of fresh coffee filled the air around camp. Finally, Sam decided it was time to wake up his buddy.

John wasn't an early riser between still working graveyards and caring for his small farm with his wife and daughter. If Sam would let him, he'd probably sleep the morning away.

John was curled up in a ball and sleeping pretty hard when Sam zipped open the door to the tent. The top of his head was the only thing visible.

"Hey, wake up, sleeping beauty. The coffee is ready."

John moaned and mumbled, "What time is it?"

"It's time to get up, it will be light soon."

"Light soon, what the hell? You said you would sleep in."

Sam laughed, "I did. I didn't get up until five."

John rolled out of the cot, fumbled around for his socks and boots, then headed out to the fire. Sam handed him a hot cup of coffee.

"Here you go; looks like it's going to be a great day."

John stretched and moaned. "Thanks, Sam."

Sam put a pot of water on the small grate next to the coffee pot and walked over to the Jeep.

"Does biscuits and gravy sound good?" he asked.

"Hell yeah, sounds great, Sam."

Opening up the food box in the Jeep, Sam grabbed two packs of freeze-dried biscuits and gravy. "I think this stuff is my favorite breakfast."

After a sip of coffee, John replied, "Mine too."

Then, after breakfast, Sam and John grabbed their day packs out of the tent, then stuffed in a few snacks, water, and an extra bag of freeze-dried food just in case. Sam packed a Jet-boil stove to boil water. Their water bladders were already full, and in their packs was enough emergency gear to get them through a cold night if something happened.

In most situations, both men always ensured they had everything they needed. Sam also left detailed maps and a time frame at home for his and John's wives in case they were late returning from the trip.

When John put on backpack, Sam noticed a can of bear spray attached to one of the front straps.

"Packing bear spray, huh?"

John smiled and adjusted the can on the strap of his pack.

"Yeah, the wife got it for me, and I told her I'd take it; I'm still packing the 44."

John's Smith & Wesson 44 magnum looked like something right out of an old Dirty Harry movie. A 44 magnum is powerful and packs a hell of a punch, especially with heavy-grain, hard-cast bullets. In the hands of someone who could use it, it can bring down any dangerous game in North America.

"What are you packing?" John asked. Sam reached into the back of the Jeep and pulled out a rifle case.

"I'm leaving the 44 in the Jeep; since we aren't going in with our heavy packs, I'm taking the 45-70."

Sam's 45-70 is a Marlin guide gun chock full of 430-grain hard-cast ammo. Capable of taking down any dangerous game animal on the planet.

"Where's your bear spray?"

Sam smiled and tapped the stock of the lever action Marlin. "Right here."

Neither man had any intention of ever using his firearm. Only as a last resort would they kill a bear when they felt their lives were in danger. John has never run into a grizzly while hunting, but Sam has.

Years ago, while Sam was hunting mule deer in western Montana's rugged Mission Mountain wilderness, Sam had just shot a monster five-point buck. Then, while field-dressing the huge buck, he heard a loud snap of a branch behind him.

When he turned, he was face to face with a charging grizzly. His rifle was leaning against a nearby tree, and there was no time to reach it. On his side, he had a can of bear spray. He sprayed a blast from the can when the bear was ten yards away.

The bear stopped and retreated, but only a short distance. Then, the massive bruin turned and charged again. Sam fired another blast of bear spray but was still unable to reach his rifle. This time, when the bear retreated, Sam ran to the nearest tree and, luckily, was able to climb high enough to escape the bear's reach. At the base of the tree, the grizzly snapped his jaws, and with terrifying growls, his claws ripped at the tree. High in the tree, Sam yelled at the bear. "Get out of here, bear, get out of here!"

Sam thought, "Please, lord, don't let him climb."

The bear finally gave up on Sam and turned to the deer. He ripped away at the loins and tore out huge hunks of flesh. Then the bear grabbed the deer by its back and, with ease, ran into the thick timber.

Horrified over the attack, Sam stayed in the tree for at least a half hour, maybe longer, before slowly clambering to the ground. Then, grabbing his rifle and pack, he scrambled back to the trail and down to his truck. "Lord, Thank You," he said out loud when he sat down inside his truck.

Even though there are plenty of cases where bear spray stops deadly encounters, Sam has never trusted just a can of bear spray since then.

The grizzly bear isn't an animal to be taken lightly in Montana. But, unfortunately, the great bear has become a menace to locals across the state, not only to outdoorsmen and campers, but to ranchers and farmers as well. Every year, they lose livestock to grizzlies that have become accustomed to an easy meal.

During bow season, bears are on the move, feeding on as much as they can in preparation for the long winter when they will seek out a den for hibernation. Unfortunately, encounters with bears have become too common and sometimes deadly for hunters, especially if you're unfortunate enough to run into a sow, dead set on protecting her cubs.

Many encounters with big bears can be avoided. But with the millions of tourists flocking to the national parks and backcountry and pressuring the bears to get that perfect selfie, an encounter, unfortunately, too often results in a mauling or the bear being killed.

John followed Sam as they hiked on the trail leading into the backcountry of the Cabinet Mountains. The trail hadn't seen any maintenance this year. Blowdowns covered the trail and made the hike even more of a challenge. Some trees were massive ponderosa pines that the two men had to leave the trail to get around. While climbing over some deadfall, John said, "This trail is a mess."

"Yeah, it is, but it's also a good sign."

"Why's that?"

"Well, hopefully, in a week, when we come back, I don't think we'll have to worry about hunters on horses," Sam replied. "Maybe we'll have the place to ourselves."

Sam and John didn't have the luxury of having horses and, too many times, had their hunts ruined by those who did. The two men would love to have horses, especially if they downed a big bull. Sam and John would be packing their game out on their backs, which Sam had done many times over the years, but he was much younger then and knew it would be rough this time.

All summer, almost every day, Sam had left his house by five a.m. Then, with a heavy pack, he'd hike four miles to prepare for this hunt. Sam knew it would be a chore but felt that even at sixty-six, he was more prepared than he had been for years.

The trail into the Cabinet Mountain wilderness is a series of long switchbacks through a thick, coniferous forest. Untouched by wildfire, large tamarack tower high towards the sky, massive pine, spruce, and fir provide homes for Stellar Jays and the famed Gray Jays (better known as Camp Robbers).

Stretches of tall bear grass line the trail, and thick patches of huckleberries are untouched by the hordes of people that flock to the vast Pacific Northwest and Rocky Mountain forest, looking to fill their gallon buckets with the sweet, wild fruit. Opening up at times, the trail wound into beautiful meadows of tall grasses and mountain wildflowers, with a grueling elevation gain of over two thousand feet before entering the wilderness.

In the back of his mind, John worried about how hard Sam pushed himself on the trail. But after years of bumming around with his good friend, he knew just how stubborn and determined he could get. Sam was setting a grueling pace up the windy trail, even with a bad knee.

When Sam stopped to check his GPS, John asked, "What's the hurry?"

"I'd like to at least get to the trailhead to the lake before ten," Sam replied.

"Well, don't go and have a heart attack on me. I'm not going to carry your ass out of here," John replied jokingly.

"I know, I know, I'm good," Sam assured John. "After we get to the trail to the lake, we have it made and can take it easy."

CHAPTER 7

At the abandoned house, Jack sat at an old table, stabbing a large hunting knife into the top, carving out chunks of wood, and flicking them on the floor. Jack and the other two fugitives are bored and getting antsy. Arguments between the men have tensions running high. Hank walked over to the table where Jack was sitting and slammed his fist on the table. "How damn long are we going to stay in this shit-hole?" he asked, glaring at Jack.

Jack jumped up, kicking the chair out from under him, then grabbed Hank by the throat and shoved him against the wall. The point of Jack's knife was pressed under Hank's chin.

"As long as I say we are. Do you have a problem with that?" Hank stared into the crazed eyes of Jack and said nothing.

"Hey, hey, come on guys, chill out," Troy urgently said while watching them from across the room. Jack glared at Troy, pressing the hunting knife harder into Hank's chin. Then, angrily, Jack said, "Do you have a problem too, Troy?"

"No, man, let's just calm down some."

Jack turned back to Hank, still pinned against the wall. Blood dripped down the blade of the knife.

"You feel me, Hank?" he teased, pressing the knife harder into Hank's chin.

"I feel ya. I feel ya."

Jack lowered the knife and pushed Hank to the side. Then he walked over, sat back down at the table, and stabbed the knife into its surface. Hank picked up a dirty old rag from the floor and held it to his chin.

"Damn, you cut me pretty deep."

Jack pulled the knife from the table and pointed it at Hank. "Next time, I'll stab it into your skull. Now sit down."

After Hank and Troy pulled their chairs to the table and sat down, they just stared at Jack.

Still carving out chunks of wood from the table, Jack said, "Now, as I see it, we have another week before things cool down around here. After that, the cops will move on. Then we can get the hell out of here." Hank wiped more blood from his chin. Troy asked if he was alright. Hank just glared at him and said. "Shut up, kid!"

Then Hank looked at Jack and asked him, "What about the car? You know they have found that couple and are looking for the car."

Jack shook his head. "Do you think I'm an idiot? We will need more supplies soon and can't use the Charger. So we'll wait until late tonight and check out some of the fancy-ass vacation homes. I know these rich assholes left a car or truck in their garage."

Later that night, the three fugitives loaded the car with all their weapons and money bags, then drove into Blake. A single streetlight lit up the convenience store parking lot. All the lights were out, and on the door hung a closed sign. The men considered breaking in but worried it would bring cops into the area. There were a few porch lights from only a small handful of houses. Blake was a ghost town after eight o'clock. After checking out a few homes north of Blake, Hank turned around and returned to the south.

A few miles down the highway, Jack spotted a paved driveway heading into the woods. A large log archway stretched across the single lane.

"Turn here," he told Hank. With the lights off, the Charger eased its way down the long driveway until it came to a steel gate with silhouettes of elk and mountains that created more of a work of art than a gate.

"These rich assholes have more money than they know what to do with," Hank proclaimed.

The gate was one of those electric keypad gates that opened when punching in a code. "What now?" asked Troy, sitting in the cramped back seat of the Charger.

"No problem," replied Jack. "Open the trunk and turn your marker lights on." Jack got out, and after fumbling around in the trunk, he appeared in front of the car, holding a tire iron.

Still sitting in the car, Troy asked Hank, "What the hell is he going to do with that?"

Hank looked at Troy in the back seat. "What do you think? These gates only keep out the honest people."

Jack walked over to the keypad, and with just a couple of blows, the back of the keypad flew off, exposing the small circuit board and a few wires. Then he ripped loose two wires and touched them together. The gate opened, and Jack waved for Hank to pull through. When Jack let go of the wires, the gate closed behind them.

The men continued down the driveway until they found a huge multi-story log home with an attached three-car garage. Everything about the place screamed money.

Hank said, "Damn, this place is crazy."

"Yeah, rich people, I hate them," Jack replied. "Hank, check out the garage, and I'll get us in the house."

Jack headed up on the massive wrap-around porch of the log home while Hank and Troy went to the garage. Troy peeked into one of the windows. "I can't see shit. It's too dark." Hank motioned for Troy to follow him. "This way, dumbass."

Hank went to the side door and kicked at it with his foot, but it didn't budge a bit. Then after slamming his shoulder against it repeatedly, he finally gave up. "Shit, It's as solid as a rock."

Disgusted, he looked around for something to use as a battering ram.

"Hang on, hang on," Troy said as he unsheathed his knife. Troy wedged the blade into the wood toward the lock and smashed the handle with a rock. Click, and the door swung open.

Troy said, "Who's the dumbass now?" Then, he laughed at Hank standing behind him, holding a big log.

Troy walked into the garage and felt against the wall for a light switch. "Jackpot," he proclaimed when the lights in the garage flicked on.

Sitting in the garage were two Polaris RZRs side by side, and next to them sat a Ford F-150 Raptor. Excited, Troy said, "Holy crap, these people do have some money!"

"Yeah, no doubt, enough that they can leave this crap to sit here all damn winter," Hank replied. Then he started looking in drawers and cabinets for the keys to the Ford. "Shit, the keys have to be here some damn where."

"Hey, Hank, check it out." Troy said, "The keys are in the side by sides."

"Yeah, so what?" What are we going to do, drive those to Canada?"

"Hell yeah, that would be awesome."

Being sarcastic, Hank glared at Troy and said, "Yeah, really awesome, you're an idiot., Let's go find Jack."

The two men left the garage and walked across the porch to the front door. A light was on inside the house. Hank said, "Well, the asshole got inside."

"I wonder how this place is like Fort Knox," Troy replied. Then he reached over, turned the doorknob, and walked into the log home.

"Hey Jack, where are you?"

"Over here, in the kitchen."

When Troy and Hank walked down the hall and into the kitchen, Jack was sitting at a giant kitchen table with his feet up and lying back with his hands folded behind his head.

"What did you find in the garage?"

Hank sat down at the table. "A Ford but no damn keys. I'll have to hot-wire it." Jack almost smiled, then tossed a set of keys over to Hank. "Here you go."

"Damn right, that will work!" Hank exclaimed. "Hey, how did you get in the house?"

Jack dangled a single key out in front of him, then slid it across the table. "With the key. It was in one of those fake rocks in a flowerpot on the porch. What dumbasses people are."

Troy asked, "Did you find anything else, Jack?"

Jack got up from the table. "Yeah, come check this shit out."

A door at the far end of the kitchen that looked like Jack had kicked open led down to a set of stairs into the basement of the house. After reaching the bottom of the stairs. Hank and Troy, at the same time, both said, "Holy shit."

"Holy shit is right," exclaimed Jack. "There is enough food and crap down here to last out World War Three!"

Hank nodded, "Damn, Jack, let's start loading some of this shit up."

"What the hell for?" Jack replied, "We're staying here; we're at least a mile off the road, and no one is around. So we'll lay low here until it's time to go."

Hank looked around, "Alright, but I don't see any beer."

"I know," Hank replied. "We may have to get some later. Take the car and, drive down to the gate, figure out how to keep it open, just in case we have to leave in a hurry."

"Why can't the kid do it?"

"Just go do it and shut up."

CHAPTER 8

In Blake, the convenience store, had just opened. A County Sheriff pulled up to the parking lot. Officer Jim Taylor had just started his shift and was ready for coffee. Inside, the store clerk had just finished brewing a fresh pot and made breakfast sandwiches in the small kitchen under the warmer.

"Good morning, sheriff. Need coffee? I just made some."

"Sounds great."

The sheriff walked over and poured a big cup, then reached into the food warmer and grabbed a breakfast sandwich. "How are these?"

The clerk smiled and said, "Well, I hate to brag, but they are the best in town."

The sheriff looked a little puzzled, "Aren't you the only place in Blake?"

"Like I said, the best in town."

Laughing the sheriff walked over to the register. "What do I owe you?"

"Nothing, it's on the house."

"Thank you. I appreciate it."

"Oh, by the way, officer, I've never seen you come through here."

"No, usually, I patrol farther south. We've been spread pretty thin with the manhunt and all."

"I heard about it on the news. Any leads yet on their whereabouts?"

"Not really; we're concentrating most of our efforts south of here, near Missoula, and up north in Lincoln County. We're looking for a black Dodge Charger."

"What! There was a black Charger here the other day."

"Did you see who was in it?"

"Sure did. A young guy mid-twenties, maybe thirty, came into the store. He was a real asshole. Had nothing but hundred-dollar bills on him."

"Was there anyone else?"

"Nope... Oh, wait a minute, there were two guys in a Jeep getting gas at the same time the asshole was."

"Did you get a good look at them?"

"Yeah, sure did, officer."

"Did one of them have a big tattoo of a swastika on the back of his neck?"

The clerk thought about it for a bit. "I don't know about the guy pumping gas, but the young man in the store didn't. He was a hell of a nice guy. Helped me out of an argument with the asshole."

"Is there anything else you can tell me about them?"

"'No, not really, that's about it."

"Which way did they go?"

"Oh, yeah, they headed toward Missoula." The clerk paused and rubbed the top of his head. "But the two in the Jeep looked like hunters. The young guy asked how far it was to Trapper Creek Road."

"Trapper Creek?"

"Yeah, about twenty miles south, maybe less. It's a horrible road that climbs up the mountain and dead ends at an old forest cabin. Only a few people know about it, let alone go up there. Anyway, have a good day, officer. Hope you catch the bastard."

When Officer Taylor returned to his truck, he sat there sipping on his coffee and eating his breakfast sandwich. "*Damn, that is good*," he thought to himself. Then he laughed and said aloud, "The best in town."

Getting on his radio, he called dispatch and reported the clerk's sighting of a black Charger heading toward Missoula a day ago. It's almost a hundred-forty miles to Missoula from Blake, with nothing in between until State Highway two-twenty which runs east thirty-five miles to Missoula, then west into Idaho. Dispatch called in the report to Missoula County and an officer was promptly dispatched toward Blake from Missoula. Officer Taylor headed south toward Highway two-twenty to meet up with the other officer somewhere along the way.

When he drove past the small Trapper Creek sign, he turned around and pulled onto the old road. Wondering about the two men in the Jeep, he thought that on the way back, he might drive up to see if the Jeep and the men were up there.

Officer Jim Taylor has only been a county sheriff for three years and made his home in Noxon, Montana, with his wife, a nurse at a small clinic in town. Three years ago, the couple had moved to Montana from New Mexico, where Jim had worked with the border patrol. While on vacation, they fell in love with Montana, especially the Noxon area. Jim enjoyed working for border patrol but had been trying to get a transfer to the northern border of Montana for a few years. However, the stress of working at the southern border and the politics that came with it was getting to be too much after several failed attempts for a transfer. So when he was offered a position with the Sanders County Sheriff's Department in Montana, Jim jumped at the opportunity.

~ ~ ~

When Sam and John reached the edge of a meadow, a small trail marker said: '*Lost Lake, one mile.*'

John asked, "Is that the lake?"

"Yeah, it sure is. There are a few lakes up around here, but Lost Lake is supposed to have some pretty good fish. A few years back, Fish and Game air-dropped a bunch of cutthroats, and I guess they've done pretty well."

Shaking his head, John asked, "How do you know all this stuff?"

"Research, lots of research. We'll hike up here tomorrow with our fly rods and give it a try."

"Are you going to be up to it?" John said with a laugh.

"Oh yeah, I'll be sore, but you just keep up."

"I'll try."

John and Sam walked over to a log, dropped their packs, and sat down with their backs against it. Then, taking off his sweatshirt, John said, "Man, it's starting to get hot."

Sam used his shirt to wipe the sweat from his forehead and said. "Yeah, it is. I bet it's at least sixty-five degrees already. On the news, they said it will hit the mid-seventies."

It's been a hot summer in Montana this year. Long stretches of triple-digit weather have set record temperatures in the valleys. Even in the mountains, the heat has been unbearable.

The fire season in the Pacific Northwest started in early March. Massive wildfires in Washington, Oregon, and California have burned hundreds of thousands of acres. As a result, thousands of homes and personal property have been lost. Smoke from the massive fires in California poured into Montana. Unfortunately, Montana also had its share of wildfires, but luckily, far fewer than the years prior.

There has been a stage two fire ban since early July. However, only a week ago, the ban was lifted, allowing the use of campfires.

From where Sam and John sat, they had an incredible view of the mountain peaks and the valley ahead, just inside the boundary of the wilderness.

The trail leveled along the ridge line and offered numerous vantage points for glassing into the open meadows and the valley below. After a mile or so, the trail began its slow descent into the valley floor before steep switchbacks made their way back up over Trapper Pass.

"Man, this is beautiful up here," John said as he reached into his backpack for a snack bar and some jerky. "Are we going up that switchback?"

"No, I don't think so," Sam replied. "We're going to hunt the valley and along the ridge line on the other side."

"Thank goodness."

Sam laughed. "I know, that would be nuts. But you can if you want."

"No thanks, I'm fine sitting right here."

Sam grabbed some meat and cheese from his pack and leaned back against the log. "Dang, I wish I would have packed in a Coke."

"I'm surprised you didn't," John replied. Then he reached into his backpack and tapped Sam on his shoulder. "Here you go, buddy."

"Holy crap, you packed in a Coke?"

"Yeah, I figured you'd be going nuts for one. So I thought I better pack in a couple for you." John didn't drink soda, but he knew how much Sam enjoyed them and figured he wouldn't pack any because of the added weight to his already-stuffed pack.

"Thanks, John, you take good care of me."

"I know, I know, just drink your damn Coke."

CHAPTER 9

The sun felt great as the two men enjoyed their break. John started sliding down lower and lower until he was flat on his back, with his head resting on his backpack. Then pulled his ball cap over his eyes. The warmth of the sun and soft grass was too much for him.

Sam looked at his friend and said, "Nap time?"

"Yeah, are we going to stay here for a bit?"

"Oh, hell yeah, just relax. I'm going to set up the spotting scope and glass the valley a bit. Then I'll probably join you."

John adjusted his cap and jokingly said, "You should. It was a hell of a climb up here for an old-timer like you."

Sam laughed and walked across the meadow to the edge of the ridge and set up the spotting scope. Then starting glassing down into the valley below, it wasn't long before Sam spotted two mule deer doe bedding down in the timber near an open meadow. Then, just a short distance from them, he spotted another: a buck sporting a dark, heavy rack. With four points per side, he was a great example of a mountain Muley and what this country had to offer a determined hunter. Sam took his rangefinder and scanned the buck. Three hundred and fifty yards. He thought, "That'd be an easy shot with his rifle."

The Cabinets were known for big Mule deer. Over the years, many Boon and Crockett bucks have come out of the high mountains of the Cabinet range. Although not a Booner buck, only a few hunters would pass up on the buck bedding down below Sam.

Sam had decided that he wouldn't harvest a Muley on this elk hunt, but on the other hand, if the opportunity for a once-in-a-lifetime Booner presented itself and came into bow range, there would be no way he could pass it up.

The spotting scope Sam was using was a 20x60 Vortex Razor mounted to a Vortex tripod. He'd bought it three weeks ago, just for the elk hunt. As Sam was zooming in on the buck, he caught a glimpse of movement out of the corner of his eye. A cow elk had walked into a small opening in the timber on the other side of the valley, maybe a hundred yards below the ridge line.

Sam quickly adjusted the spotting scope and turned it towards the cow. Once he found the elk in the scope, he scanned the timber. Another cow appeared, then another. After that, Sam started seeing even more elk bedding in the thick trees. He counted at least ten cows in the timber. Then Sam spotted a small raghorn bull easing its way toward the cows, followed closely by a five-by-five bull.

Sam looked over at John and could hear him snoring away.

"Crap, he's out like a light." He wanted to avoid getting up and running at the risk of being spotted by a suspicious cow. So Sam picked up some small stones and tossed them close to John. Finally, one stone landed close, but John adjusted his feet and pulled his hat farther down over his eyes.

"Damn it," Sam whispered to himself, then grabbed a little bit bigger rock and tossed it. "Crap," he said as the rock hit his buddy right in the nuts. But it worked, and John quickly clutched his crotch and rolled over in pain.

Sam couldn't help laughing when John glared at him. Then he motioned him over and held his hands above his head. whispering, "Elk!" He then motioned again for him to stay low.

Once John reached Sam and sat beside him, Sam handed him the spotting scope.

"Sorry about your nuts," he laughed.

"Yeah, nice shot," John replied, shaking his head and smiling.

Sam pointed across the ridge and said, "Check it out. There's a bunch of elk." Having just materialized out of the timber, you could now see some elk moving into open areas along the ridge with your naked eye.

John focused the spotting scope and glassed over at the elk. "Damn, that is one helluva bull."

"Yeah, he's a five-point, and there's another rag horn."

John replied, "Not that one. This one is a monster."

Sam grabbed his binoculars and looked at the elk clearing into an open cut in the timber. "Holy crap, that's the herd bull, I bet."

The bull was big. Its massive rack had seven long points on each side and more than forty inches of spread. Its rack was heavy and thick. John and Sam were looking at a world-class bull that didn't have a clue he was being watched.

Although the two men had hunted elk together, it had been over ten years since Sam had filled his elk tag. John has never shot an elk or been up close to a dead one. John had a chance during rifle season with Sam a few years back. But 'buck fever' caused a hurried shot, and he missed—something Sam never lets him forget.

John asked. "How in the hell are we going to get something that big out of here?"

"It's going to be a bitch, we'll have to make a lot of trips with our packs, and we'll have to do it fast." Sam said, "In this heat, the meat will spoil quick."

Sam had packed a lot of game on his back over the years and knew just how hard it could be. But, unless you had horses or mules, you had little choice.

Sam and John sat on the ridge and watched the elk ease its way down to Trapper Creek. A few more cows, calves, and a decent six-by-six bull joined the herd. Sam and John counted over twenty elk in the valley below.

"There's no sense in going any further," Sam said. "We'll just hang out here and watch for a while."

John agreed. "Yeah, I think we found them."

Both men gave each other a fist bump, then suddenly, John said, "Hey, look, there's a big Mule deer buck."

"Oh yeah, I forgot about him," Sam chuckled.

John whispered, "Damn, He's pretty nice."

"I know, but we aren't in here for him."

"What do you think, Sam?" John asked, "Do you think the elk will be here next week?"

"I don't see why not. They'll be here as long as they aren't pressured and spooked out of here. With the trail's condition, I don't think we have to worry about horses. I didn't even see any old horse crap on the trail," Sam assured John.

"Me neither. Plus, I think we're the only ones stupid enough to climb this far up that trail."

"I hear ya."

The area John and Sam had drawn their tags is vast. Only a handful of tags are available each year, a once in a lifetime draw. This is one of the reasons your chances of harvesting a trophy bull are good.

Sam and John drawing the tags the same year was nothing less than a miracle. It just doesn't happen.

Sam is sure that other bow hunters who drew the same or cow-only tag would be hunting down lower and closer to the vast areas of private land with resident elk herds year-round, moving back and forth from bordering state and forest lands. At least, he hoped so! A hunter with a coveted bighorn sheep or mountain goat tag might venture into the area—Maybe. But Sam knew hunting for them was better miles south of him and John.

Soon, Sam and John grabbed their backpacks and eased a little farther along the ridge to a spot that offered more cover. The elk mingled in the open meadows near the creek for at least an hour before returning to the timber.

"I could sit here until dark, but we better start heading back," Sam said.

"Sounds good, Sam. Pretty exciting, isn't it?"

"Oh yeah, I'm pumped," Sam said as they crept back over to the log, then glanced over the valley before heading down the trail.

"Well, one thing for sure, it's all downhill from here," John said as he handed Sam his trekking poles.

"I'll need these for sure. Downhill is a lot harder on my dang knee."

"I bet. Are you still planning on getting a knee replacement after hunting season?"

"I think so. After my last surgery, the doctor told me that's what I'll need."

"Hell yeah, you'll be like a new man. I'll never keep up!"

Sam laughed and headed down the trail. When they got to the sign for Lost Lake, they stopped and looked down the trail. It wasn't much more than a game trail.

John said, "Nice, only one mile down."

Sam chuckled and said, "Yep, and one mile back up."

The two men were making good time despite Sam having to stop a lot more going down than he did coming up because of his knee.

"Knee hurting you?"

"A little, but I'm good." John knew it was more than a little, but Sam would never admit it.

Sam and John returned to their camp earlier than expected and had plenty of time to unwind before dark. Sam dropped his pack, set it up on the Jeep's hood, then unlocked the driver's side door and put his 45-70 across the seats. "I'm not packing that thing tomorrow. It's pretty damn heavy."

"I bet the ammo alone has to weigh five pounds."

"Probably does."

"It didn't slow you down any. You flew down the trail."

Sam smiled. "Yeah, a man on a mission."

"Are we eating freeze-dried food tonight, Sam?"

"Hell no, my wife made a killer beef stew. All I have to do is warm it up. Are you ready to eat?"

John was starving but said, "I could eat, but it's up to you."

Sam walked over and sat in a camp chair. "How about we kick back and relax a bit? You look worn out."

Before John went to take a seat, Sam asked, "How about grabbing me a Coke out of the cooler?"

"You bet. Anything else?"

"Nah, I'm good. Thanks, buddy."

John walked over to the Jeep, grabbed an ice-cold Coke for Sam and a blue Powerade for himself, then sat in a camp chair. "It's been a helluva day, Sam."

"Yeah, pretty awesome. Thanks for being up here with me."

"No place I'd rather be, buddy."

It wasn't long before Sam was up building a fire. John asked, "Need help?"

"Nope, just relax. I want to get some hot coals for dinner."

Sitting around the fire, they talked about seeing all the elk and how thankful they were to be there, sitting next to a warm fire in the middle of nowhere. John said, "I love this stuff."

Sam kicked his feet up on a stump of wood and replied, "Me too, John."

CHAPTER 10

Meanwhile, Officer Taylor had met up with the other officer out of Missoula and was returning to Blake. He couldn't quit thinking about the men in the Jeep. Then he thought to himself it was probably nothing. But when he reached Trapper Creek, he decided to drive up the road just in case.

"Damn, this road is bad," he said out loud as the Ford F-150 bounced across the rocky road, then thought to himself, "*I should have found out how far it is to the cabin.*"

It was dark when he reached the top of the last switchback. In the distance, he could see the glow of a campfire. Suddenly, he started feeling a little eerie. Once again, he thought, "*Hmm, nobody knows I'm up here. Maybe I should call in. But, Nah, it's probably just a couple of hunters, like the store clerk said.*"

Sam had just finished serving his wife's killer beef stew at the camp. John slammed it down like he hadn't eaten in days. "Damn, that was delicious."

"Thanks, I'll let the wife know. There's plenty more."

Suddenly, John spotted headlights coming up the road. "What the hell."

Sam stood up. "Who in the hell would be coming up here at dark?"

"Not sure. Do you think it could be someone heading to the cabin?"

"I don't know. I don't like it."

Sam walked to the Jeep and opened the door to get his handgun.

When John spotted the light bar on the truck and 'Sanders County Sheriff' printed in bold letters on the side. He said, "Hey Sam, it's a sheriff."

"What? I hope everything is okay." Both men immediately got concerned, thinking something might be wrong at home.

Sam placed his handgun on the Jeep's front bumper and walked back over to the fire.

When Officer Taylor approached the camp and stepped out of the truck, John said, "Hi, officer, I hope everything is okay." Officer Taylor could tell immediately that both men looked concerned and worried about him being there.

"Everything is fine. Nothing to worry about," Officer Taylor assured the two men.

Relieved, Sam replied, "Thank God, I was scared something had happened at home." Once again, Officer Taylor assured Sam that everything was alright as he approached to the fire.

"Sorry, I'm sure you're a little surprised to see me up here."

"Yeah, more than a little. What's going on?" Sam replied.

"The store clerk back in Blake told me you guys may be up here."

Sam shrugged his shoulders; and asked, "Yeah, so why did you drive all the way up here?"

John sat down by the fire, but Sam remained standing. John could tell that Sam was a little pissed off now and hoped he would keep it under control.

There were too many times at work when John had seen Sam get pissed, especially when one of the bosses would have ridiculous suggestions or questioned what he did all night.

Sam had a short fuse and was blunt about sharing his thoughts. So often, John would have to step in and try to calm things down. But unfortunately, it didn't always work. But that's one of the things John respected about Sam. When he was right, he was right, and he never put up with any bullshit.

Officer Taylor could sense the slight tension in Sam's voice, but he had driven up there for a reason. "What are your names?"

"I'm Sam, Sam Conners, and this is my friend John Turner."

"Well, Mr. Conners, I'm sure I startled you driving up here, but could I see your I.D.?" Sam reached into the cargo pocket of his pants and handed the officer his driver's license.

"I'm still wondering why you're here, officer."

Officer Taylor turned to John, who already had his license, and handed it to the officer. Then, after looking at it with his flashlight, he handed it back.

"Thank you, Mr. Turner."

The tension from the officer's surprise visit had become more relaxing as the officer shined his light on the Jeep license plate. "You're both from Flathead County?"

Sam replied, "Yes, sir., We live in the Kalispell and Columbia Falls area."

"I'm Officer Jim Taylor of the Sanders County Sheriff's Department. Have you two heard about the armed robberies in Spokane?"

"Yes, have they been caught?" asked Sam

"Not yet. We have reason to believe the three men have made their way into Montana. I understand you may have seen a man driving a black Dodge Charger."

Sam said. "Oh yeah, a guy in his late twenties was at the store in Blake. He was a real piece of work."

"Yeah, a real asshole," added John.

"Can you tell me anything about him or the car, Mr. Turner? The clerk in the store told me that you helped to de-escalate an argument between himself and the guy at the counter."

"Yeah, all he had was hundreds, and I gave him some change."

"Is there anything else? Tattoos or scars you might have noticed?"

"No, nothing I could see. He looked like a normal guy except for being a dick. He just threw his money on the counter and left."

"How about you, Mr. Conner? Where were you?"

"I was outside filling up the Jeep. I commented on the Charger, and the guy just cussed me out. He was in a hurry, didn't waste time pulling away, and headed south."

"Towards Missoula?"

"Yes, sir, he headed south and wasn't wasting time, either."

"Is there anything else, Mr. Conner? Did you notice the plates?"

"Yeah, Idaho plates, but I didn't pay attention to the number. Although now that I think about it, there was a sticker on the rear window, a man and a woman, plus a dog. You know, one of those stick figure stickers you see on minivans. I thought it looked really out of place on that car."

Officer Taylor reached out and shook both the men's hands.

"Again, I apologize for interrupting you at your camp."

Sam said, "No problem, I'm surprised you made it up here in that Ford!"

The officer laughed and said, "I know. I wish the department had Chevys."

John said, "Here we go again, Chevy guys!" Sam and the officer laughed.

"Well, Mr. Turner, it did make it up here."

Right away, Sam spoke up. "Yeah, but you have to make it back down. Good luck!"

Officer Taylor asked, "By the way, how long are you guys camping?"

"We're hiking into Lost Lake to do some fishing in the morning," said John, "then packing up the next day."

"We'll be back next weekend for the opening day of bow season," said Sam. "We have the forest cabin up the road rented for ten days. So if you're in the area, you're welcome to come up and shoot the shit."

"I may take you up on that. You guys take care, and good luck fishing."

The officer got in his truck and went back down the beat-up forest road.

Sam looked at John. "That was different. I didn't expect that."

"Me neither, but he was a pretty cool cop."

Sam and John settled back into their chairs next to the campfire. "Well, where was I, John?"

"You were bullshitting about some hunt."

"It's not bullshit."

John chuckled. "I know, Sam. I know."

CHAPTER 11

The following day, Sam zipped open the tent. "Rise and shine, hillbilly. Time to get going."

John replied, "Alright, what time is it?"

"The sun's up, and I slept in. Breakfast and coffee's ready."

When John stepped out of the tent, Then put his arms above his head and took a big stretch. Sam laughed when John's t-shirt pulled up over his belly.

"Nice gut."

John patted his belly, "Yes sir, solid steel and sex appeal."

"Yeah, right." Sam handed his buddy a cup of coffee.

A skillet full of scrambled eggs, chopped potatoes, and sausage was on the grate over the fire. "Are you hungry?"

"Hell yeah." Sam dished out a huge plate and handed it to John.

"You know Sam, you're one helluva camp cook."

"Thanks, Buddy, eat up."

Sam sat down next to the fire and rubbed his knee.

"Your knee hurting you, Sam?"

"A little bit, but I'm used to it."

After breakfast, the two men gathered up their fly rods and backpacks. "Are you packing the 45-70 again?" asked John

"No, I'm taking the forty-four."

Sam had a Smith and Wesson model 329PD 44 mag. The scandium alloy frame and titanium cylinder made it lightweight and much easier to pack than the heavy Marlin. Sam wore a chest holster that got the gun off his hip and put it in a perfect position should he need it quickly.

Sam said, "I don't know why I took the rifle yesterday."

"Me neither," John replied.

Sam grabbed his trekking poles and led the way to the trailhead. Once again, John followed close behind. While climbing up the long switchbacks, Sam stopped a lot. Not because he was tired, but in his head, all he was thinking about was the giant herd bull. He told John about different scenarios of how they would set up to get the big bull into bow range.

"I won't pass up a six-point, but I really want that herd bull."

"I know," John said. "I think you'll have a good chance."

After John had missed his shot on a bull during the previous season, he'd made it clear to Sam that the next shot was his. Even though Sam agreed, he always told John that if he had a good clear shot, he should take it.

Once John and Sam reached the trail marker to Lost Lake and started the one-mile descent to the remote mountain lake, their excitement grew as they headed down the narrow trail.

Along the way, several mule deer bounced down the trail in front of the two men before disappearing into the timber. Then, just a little farther along the trail, John spotted a decent Muley buck. "Sam, check it out, a buck," he whispered.

"Sweet, He's a good buck," Sam whispered back.

"Not like that one you spotted yesterday, Sam, but he's a shooter, alright."

The buck just stood motionless as they walked by.

Sam stopped and looked back at the buck," Yeah, we might have to do some deer hunting if we fill our elk tags early."

"Damn right, that would be awesome," John replied.

Soon, the tree line below them started opening up, and the two men could see the sun glistening off the lake's crystal-clear water.

"We're almost there, John." Sam proclaimed, "Not far now."

It was amazing when they cleared the timber and could see the whole lake. A rocky shoreline stretched almost entirely around the lake. At one end, rocky cliffs reached high above the water. Deep down in the clear water, boulders broken away from the cliffs years ago dotted the bottom of the lake. A small stream made its way through the tall grass at the other end of the lake. The tall pine and fir threw a perfect reflection on the water.

Sam sat on a large rock close to the water's edge.

"Holy Crap, this is beautiful," John said while scrambling to set up his fly rod. "Now, if there's fish, it will be perfect."

"Get with it, buddy. I'm going to sit on this rock, have a Coke, and take it all in. Save some fish for me."

Sam just sat there in awe at just how beautiful it was. The warm sun on his face and not a cloud in the sky. He thought, "*Wow, what a perfect place for a cabin, everything you need is already right here.*"

"Fish on!" echoed across the lake. Sam turned to see John knee-deep in the water, his fly rod bent and a cutthroat trout thrashing in the air. "Damn, I forgot my net, Sam."

"I'm coming. Hang in there," Sam replied. When he approached John, he noticed his hiking boots and socks lying on the shore. John was standing knee-deep and barefoot in the water. "Dang, hillbilly, didn't you pack in your wading boots?"

"Nope, I forgot them at home. Toss me the net," John gently landed the cutthroat.

"Hey, let me get a picture before you release it." Sam took his phone out of his pocket and snapped a few pictures. "Nice. That's a beautiful fish."

"Thanks. Are you going to start fishing, too?"

"You bet," Sam said, "but I'm putting on my dang wading boots."

The two men worked their way along the shoreline. Again and again, cutthroats rose to take the well-placed flies. Then, Sam watched a huge trout rise from the rocks in the crystal-clear water to strike his fly. "Fish On," he yelled out to John.

"Is he a nice one?"

"Oh yeah, my biggest yet!" After landing the trout and holding it up to show John, John hollered, "Do you want a picture?" John was quite a ways down the shoreline. He was still standing barefoot in the cold water.

"I'll get it," Sam replied. Then he reached into his pocket for his phone while trying to gently hold the trout in one hand just as he lined up for his selfie. *Splash*, the big trout gave a flip and escaped. John heard Sam say a loud "Crap!" then, laughing, he said, "I would have come over and taken the picture, you know."

"I know, maybe next time. But I did get a nice picture of the splash."

After the fishing slowed, Sam went along the rocky shoreline to John, sat on the rocks, grabbed the flattest rock he could find, and set up his stove.

"Time for lunch?" John asked.

"Yeah, I'm pretty hungry."

"Sounds good to me. I'm ready, too."

Sam laughed while watching his barefoot buddy painfully walk out of the lake to his hiking boots. "You know, wading boots were on the list I gave you."

"Yeah, I know. I didn't look at the list."

"That figures."

John joined Sam on the rocks beside the stove. "Sam, this place is awesome and full of fish."

"Yep, good times."

After finishing lunch, Sam took his fly rod and headed down the shore toward the rocky cliff. "I'm going to give it a try over by the rocks."

"Sounds good, Sam. I think I'll relax for a bit."

"Yeah, it's getting pretty hot. So the fishing may slack off," Sam replied.

Just before the cliff, there was a small sandy beach, and when Sam got there, he noticed bear tracks and told John to come check it out.

"What is it?"

"It's bear tracks. A grizzly."

The tracks in the sand were easy to make out. Claw marks sunk deep into the sandy ground at the end of the front paws, making it easy to tell it was a grizzly that had made the tracks.

John got up, walked over to where Sam was standing, and glanced down at the tracks. "Well, hell, that sucks."

"Yeah, no shit. We'll have to be careful when we're hunting. Especially if we down an elk."

A grizzly has a keen sense of smell, over two thousand times better than a human's. With such an acute sense of smell, they can smell rotting carcasses of animals and, much worse, a gut pile almost twenty miles away. In addition, grizzlies eat just about everything, from nuts and fruit to hoofed animals. So Sam and John knew that, for a lurking grizzly, a fresh gut pile was like ringing a dinner bell.

"If we get an elk, every time we make a return trip to pack it out, one of us will have to keep watch as the other loads the packs," Sam said.

"Yeah, a close watch," John replied. "After hearing that story of your encounter, I think about that shit all the time."

"We'll be fine, buddy. I was flying solo on that hunt. Not too damn smart on my part. The wife still gets pissed when I go out by myself."

"Well, shit, can you blame her?"

"No, but I won't sit around and wait until you can get the time off!"

"Yeah, I wish I was retired."

Sam laughed. "Just thirty more years."

"Don't remind me."

John looked at the sun and said, "Damn, it's getting frickin' hot."

"I know. I'm thinking about taking a quick swim."

"That water is pretty cold, but I'm game if you are," John replied.

Sam and John stripped down to their shorts and waded into the knee-deep water. "Well, jump in, buddy," said John, looking at Sam. "It was your idea. You go first."

Sam looked at the cliff and told John, "Hey, I've got a better idea. Let's climb up to that ledge and jump in."

"What the hell, are you nuts?"

"No, it's only twenty feet up and plenty deep. Back in the day, my nephew and I used to jump off sixty feet at Tally Lake."

"Yeah, back in the day. You aren't a spring chicken anymore, Sam."

"I know. That's why I don't want to go to the top."

"You're crazy, Sam."

Sam just laughed and started climbing the cliff. Once out on the ledge, he told John. "Well, here I go."

"Go for it, you crazy old fart."

Without hesitation, Sam jumped and yelled, "Geronimo!" Then, after a big splash, he plunged ten feet into the crystal-clear water and swam back up to the top.

"How was it?" John asked.

"Damn! It's not bad. Feels great." John had already started climbing up the ledge. He knew Sam would never let him live it down if he didn't jump.

Splash, John plunged into the cold water. "Holy shit, It's frickin' cold. You said it wasn't bad."

Standing up in the sand, drying off with his sweatshirt, Sam was laughing his ass off. "Sorry buddy, I guess I lied."

Then Sam walked over to his backpack and pulled out a pair of hiking pants and undershorts.

"What the hell, Sam? You said nothing about bringing spare clothes."

Again, Sam laughed, then replied. "You should have looked at the list."

After changing, Sam said, "Well, we might as well start heading back. We still have to pack up camp and get home."

"Sounds good, Sam."

CHAPTER 12

Patrol cars fill the street in front of a two-story home in a suburb on the south end of Seattle, Washington. The local law enforcement is holding back crowds of people and reporters. Vehicles from the State Crime Lab sit in the driveway. A single black SUV sat at the curb in front of the house.

Special Agent Dan Black stands inside the home with his hand covering his mouth and nose. Two bodies lie in the kitchen, surrounded by puddles of dried blood covering the floor. Upstairs in the bathroom, another body lies face-down halfway in the shower, with at least five stab wounds in his back.

The bodies have been there for days, and the stench from the bodies is sickening. All three male victims had been stabbed repeatably, and each had a stab wound under his chin, piercing into his skull. The horrific scene of the violent murders is the last known address of Jack Bishop.

From the basement, an officer yells up the stairs, "Agent Black, somebody get Agent Black!" When Dan made his way over to the head of the stairs and looked down at the officer, the officer said, "You better see this, agent" At the bottom stairs, Dan could see a desk tucked away in the far corner. "It's all there, Agent."

"All what?"

"Plans about the armed robberies in Spokane." When Agent Black approached the desk, pictures of all the businesses targeted in the robberies in Spokane were scattered on top of the desk. In addition, on the wall were pictures of several armored transport vehicles, along with detailed maps of their routes.

Dan turned to the officer and told him not to let anybody into the basement before he could get his team there. Then he reached into his pocket for his phone and called the number to his office.

T.J. answered, "Hey Dan, how's it look over there?"

"It's bad, real bad. Three men were murdered and have been dead for a long time. The damn stink is horrible. There's more, though, I'm in the basement, and there's all kinds of evidence about those robberies in Spokane. You'd better send the team over. Tell them to hurry."

"Sure thing Dan, right away. Oh yeah, and Dan? Go get some fresh air."

"Yeah, right, just get them here."

Dan Black is a ten-year veteran of the FBI based in Seattle, Washington. Shortly after leaving the Air Force as a combat intelligence officer, he became the lead investigator and team leader for a special tactical unit.

Dan's team is tasked to cover some of the most violent crimes and homicides in the Pacific Northwest. He transferred to the unit from Los Angeles and made his home outside Seattle with his wife and two kids. In his late forties, Dan is clean-cut. His straight chin and focused eyes give him a demanding look of confidence.

Outside the home, Dan sits in his SUV, waiting for his team members to arrive. On his phone, Dan is being briefed about the details of the armed robberies in Spokane and the manhunt by Tanner Jones.

Tanner, a desk jockey, is the most vital member of Dan's four-person team. He's one of the best at his job, an expert in crime and intelligence analysis, going on twenty years with the FBI. He sits in front of four monitors in his office, digging into every little detail of violent crimes.

Dan is now confident that Jack Bishop was one of the fugitives in the robberies and now a murder suspect in the triple homicide. "Get me a plane, T.J. I'm going to Spokane, and send me everything we have on Jack Bishop."

When the charter plane landed in Spokane the following day, then taxied to a small hangar, Agent Dan Black was met by the Captain of the Spokane County Sheriff's Department.

"Agent Black, I'm Captain Don Anderson. How was your flight?"

"It was good, Captain. I take it you know why I'm here?"

Shaking hands, Captain Anderson replied, "Yes, sir, I believe I do."

"Good, but the first thing you can do is drop the 'sir.'"

The Captain nodded. "Understood. Am I taking you to the FBI headquarters downtown?"

"No, I'm going to your station."

"Alright, get in."

The ride to the station was quiet. Agent Black just stared at his phone, reading page after page of reports from his office in Seattle. Then, after finally arriving at the station, the two men walked up the stairs and passed through two large, heavy glass doors.

"This way, my office is over here." Dan followed the Captain into the office, then closed the door behind him. "Mr. Black, can I call you Mr. Black? Or do you prefer Agent?"

"Neither. I'm going to be here for a while. You can call me Dan."

"Very well, Dan. How can I and my department be of assistance?"

"Well, first off, I'm going to need an office, and there has to be a spare coffee pot around here somewhere."

"What else?"

"I'll need absolutely everything you have about the robberies, and I will have to meet with everyone involved in the investigation."

"Everyone?"

"Yes, everyone, including any witnesses to the robberies."

"Alright, I'll get to work on it."

"Thank you, Captain."

"In the meantime, Dan, in the break room down the hall, there's a couple of vending machines, and there is always a fresh pot of coffee. You look like you can use some. So make yourself at home."

Suddenly Dan's phone rang. "I've got to take this. Thanks again, captain."

Dan grabbed his phone from his pocket. The call was from T.J. "Hi T.J., what do you have for me?"

"Hey Dan. I've got plenty. I'm sending everything to you. Do you have your laptop?"

"I do, but go ahead and tell me."

"We identified the victims: all three are low-level Broken Cross gang members, each with a long list of priors, mainly petty theft. Nothing stands out."

"What about downstairs in the basement?"

"Yeah, that's where it gets interesting. We pulled prints, and they all came up belonging to Jack Bishop and Hank Barnes. We also recovered all kinds of info from the busted-up hard drive we found outside in the trash. Bishop was definitely one of the three guys who hit that armored transport there in Spokane."

Dan replied, "Yeah, I figured that."

"We also came up with the address of Jose Garcia, a suspected lowlife gun dealer outside of Portland with ties to the Broken Cross. We sent the locals there early this morning. The guy was dead, beaten to death with a baseball bat. There was also a stash of class-three weapons and ammo. It looks like whoever killed Jose made off with some heavy weapons."

"Damn, T.J., this shit is getting worse and worse."

"Jose had cameras set up all over the place."

"What did you find, T.J.?"

"I'm still waiting for them to send over the video. When I get it, I'll forward it to you."

"Thanks, T.J., go get some rest. You've had a long night."

"What about you, Dan, getting any sleep?"

"No, not much. Great job, T.J."

"All in a day's work, Dan, well, all in a night's work, anyways. Just be careful."

"Always, T.J."

CHAPTER 13

An officer opened the door to the captain's office. "Excuse me, Agent Black. We've got an office ready for you, and the two detectives in the investigation are on their way here."

"Perfect, Lead the way."

Tucked away in a corner office of the station was a single desk; a printer, a lamp, and a phone sat on top. On the wall hung a decent-sized marker board. In the corner was a fold-out table with a coffee pot, a can of Folgers coffee, and some styrofoam cups.

"It's not much, Agent."

"It's fine. Where can I find some water?"

"Just down the hall. There's a water dispenser."

"Alright, thank you."

After making a pot of coffee, Dan set up his laptop and started downloading everything sent over from the Seattle office.

When his phone rang, it was T.J. "Hey T.J., what do you have for me?

"I got the video from Jose Garcia's place. It was Hank Barnes. We checked into possible connections to Bishop, who was imprisoned on the same block. He got released just a couple of days before Bishop did."

"Good work T.J."

"We also pulled another set of prints off a beer bottle in the basement here in Seattle. They belong to a Troy Becker. He was also on the same block as Bishop and got released the day after Bishop."

"Damn, T.J., looks like you nailed down the three assholes in the robberies over here. Send over all you got and stay on it."

"You bet, Dan. You should be getting everything any minute."

"Thanks, T.J."

Dan started printing page after page of T.J.'s report and the mug shots of Bishop, Barnes, and Becker. While staring at the mug shots, he took a marker and wrote their names on the pictures. Then, talking out loud to himself, he said. "BBB. Bishop, Barnes and Becker." Then he thought, "*What do you know, Triple B's?* The damn press will have a field day with that shit."

Just then, there was a knock at Dan's door. The two detectives had finally arrived at the station. "Come in, detectives. I'm Agent Dan Black. But before you get started with that 'agent' stuff, you can call me Dan. I don't care for that formal crap."

"Sounds good, Dan. I'm Detective Rick Peters, the lead investigator on the robberies, and since we're going by first names, Rick will do. This is Karen Levitt, my partner on the investigations."

Karen said, "Pleasure to meet you, Dan."

"You too, Karen. Is Karen alright?"

"Yes, it's fine with me, Dan."

'Alright, now that we've got that done, have a seat."

"Have you both been briefed by your captain on why I'm setting up shop here?"

Rick replied, "A little, but I think he decided to leave the details to you."

"Well, the robbery is now a murder investigation. There are three dead in Seattle and another just outside of Portland. We have solid evidence that Jack Bishop is responsible for the murders in Seattle and is the so-called mastermind of the robberies here in Spokane. We've identified three suspects: Jack Bishop, Hank Barnes, and Troy Becker."

Dan paused and handed Rick a picture of Jose Garcia.

Then Dan continued, "We've got video of Hank Barnes beating Jose Garcia, a low-life arms dealer, to death with a baseball bat in his home," Dan continued. "He also got away with three class three weapons, three Glocks, and one hell of a lot of ammo. I've alerted the ATF, and they're sending an agent to join our team."

Rick interrupted him. "Damn, it sounds like we've got some bad-ass fugitives."

"Yeah, that's why me and my team in Seattle are taking the lead on this. I want everything from here on out to go through us." Dan said, "I'll give you the detailed reports from my team, don't you worry. In the meantime, I need to know everything you have about the robberies. I want these assholes bad."

Rick picked up the mug shots of the three men, then handed one to Karen. "Look familiar?"

"Yeah, sure does. That's the guy in Blake."

Dan said, "Alright, tell me about him, Karen."

"This guy was caught on camera at a convenience store in Blake, Montana," she said. "He was driving a black Dodge Charger that matched a car stolen during a home invasion in Idaho outside Priest River, near where the three suspects abandoned the pickup. The couple in the home were found tied up a day after it went down."

"Was Becker alone?"

"Yeah, as far as we know, Officer Jim Taylor, a Sanders County sheriff, talked to the store owner working when this guy was in the store. The officer sent us his report and the video. It looks like Becker and the Charger were heading to Missoula. Taylor also talked to a Sam Conner and John Turner, who were at the store at the same time."

Dan said, "Where are those guys now?"

Rick said, "They were camped up a road fifteen, maybe twenty miles south of Blake. A place called Trapper Creek. There probably back home by now."

"Did they check out?"

"Yeah, just a couple of guys up there scouting for an elk hunt. They're clean."

"Is there anything more about Becker, Rick?"

"Yeah, Becker looks like the guy we got on a video from one of the places hit a day before the robberies. Gold, Silver, and Loan, over on Rollins Avenue. He was wearing a ball cap pulled down over his eyes. We suspected it was the same guy in Blake, but we couldn't be sure."

Dan leaned back in his chair and crossed his arms, "What about the day of the robbery? Since there was a camera, what about that video?"

"Nothing, these guys knew what they were doing. The camera caught the first guy coming in the front door and shooting the camera with a paintball gun. It was quick, and we only got one guy with a black ski mask, hoodie, and gloves. It only took a second to take out the camera. As I said, they knew what they were doing."

"How about witnesses?"

"None—the place was empty except for the owner. They smashed him in the face with the butt of a rifle. Then one guy handed him a note saying that he had thirty seconds to open the safe or he'd cut his throat. Needless to say, he opened the safe. No one said a single word the whole time."

"What about outside, anybody, any cameras?"

"There was one drunken homeless guy in the alley, but he didn't hear or see a thing. Not many cameras in that part of town."

"So that's it?"

"I'm afraid so."

"What about the pawn shop? They always have cameras."

"Yeah, plenty, but they weren't recording when the place got hit."

"Well, that figures. What else? Any witnesses?"

"Just two employees, The same as before, the place was empty. Two guys in masks and hoodies busted in the front door. Then the other one came in through the back. Same kind of note. It was quick. They hit the safe after smashing the shit out of the employees' faces. Nobody said a word. When they were finished, they all went out the back."

"Was there anybody out front when it went down?"

"Yeah, five local gang-bangers. They said they didn't see a thing. We brought them in, but they were tight-lipped. We had to let them go."

"Jesus, I can't believe it. Not even one law-abiding bystander with a damn cell phone."

Karen looked disgusted and said, "Nope, but let a cop pull someone over, and everyone starts filming."

Dan agreed with Karen and said, "Alright, what about the armored transport? That was the last thing that got hit, right?"

Rick replied, "Yeah, but these guys had it all planned out good. They hit a casino during cash out. The dumbass driver parked the transport in the back, waiting for the two guards to come out with the money bags. They didn't stand a chance. Both were hit with bats on the back of the head and went out like a light. One guard is still in critical condition at Saint Peter's. When the other guard came around, there was no one around."

Dan said. "Alright, a casino. Surely they had cameras recording everything."

Rick shook his head and said, "Well, usually that's true, but a technician was working on the securing system, and he had the whole system down. Including all the cameras."

"You've got to be kidding me. A little bit of a coincidence. Did you pull the technician in?"

"No, we didn't."

Dan looked surprised, "Get him picked up and bring him in now. If you can find him, he probably isn't a legit tech. I bet he's part of it and is in the wind."

Rick called a sheriff into the office. "Get with the city and head over to Valley Security. Find out who they had working at River Bend Casino when the robbery went down. Find the guy and bring him in."

"Yes, sir, detective."

"Okay, Rick, where were we? What about the damn truck?"

"Well, we did have a little luck at the casino. A half a block away from the robbery, a camera at a bank got video of three guys wearing hoodies in an older Chevy pickup. We ran the plates, and they came up reported stolen. But, of course, you already know the rest about what happened north along the Idaho border."

"Yeah, I know about it. What about the sheriff involved, did he I.D. our guys?"

"Nope, he was too busy dodging gunfire."

"Alright, we know who these assholes are now anyways. I hoped they made a mistake at one of the robberies, but it doesn't look like they did. But they sure screwed up at the murder scenes. So they'll make another mistake, and we'll be right there to catch them when they do."

Looking down at a map, Dan said. "It looks like I'll be heading to Missoula soon. How far is Blake from there?"

Rick said, "I'm not sure, northwest, hundred and thirty miles, maybe a little more."

"What do they have there?"

"Not much, just the one store, a small motel, and a bunch of summer vacation homes. Most everyone is gone now. Getting their kids back in school and whatnot."

Dan looked at a couple of maps while rubbing his chin.

"That's interesting. You say most search efforts are mainly concentrated in Missoula and Missoula County."

"Yeah, plus many resources have been directed to Lake County, Montana, near the Canadian border and the panhandle of Idaho.

"Hmmm. We may need to look in the right places.

"Okay, detectives, let's start getting every little piece together. I need everything you told me on a timeline and all the details. I don't care how small, put it together in a report, package it up, and send it to Agent Tanner Jones at my office in Seattle. ASAP!

"Right away, Dan. We'll have it ready within the hour."

"Good enough, detectives, Thank you."

Dan picked up his phone after the detectives left the office and called T.J.

"T.J., there's a change of plans. You're going to be receiving all the reports on the robberies. I need you to review everything and alert me to anything you find."

"No problem, Dan. So, what's the change of plans?"

"I'm done here, and I want everything sent to the Missoula field office."

"Well, that was quick. I guess you're going to Montana?"

"Yeah, I have a hunch everyone is looking in the wrong places."

"Anything else, Dan?"

"Yeah, there is a small town up in the mountains of Montana called Blake. I need the latest satellite imagery and maps of the whole area. Also, get Jake and Wyatt on a plane to Missoula."

"Right away, Dan."

"Thanks, T.J."

CHAPTER 14

An army veteran, Jake Kellar was a First Lieutenant and platoon leader with the Fourth Ranger Battalion based out of Fort Benning, Georgia.

Assigned to his platoon was automatic rifleman Wyatt Carter. Both men had spent two deployments at Bagram Air Base in the Parwan Province of Afghanistan.

Jake and Wyatt left the army and were later accepted into the FBI academy at Quantico, Virginia. After graduating and being assigned to different headquarters, they teamed up again in Seattle after being hand chosen by Agent Dan Black.

Both men are just over six feet, and it's easy to tell they spend a lot of time at the gym. Jake and Wyatt carry themselves with sureness and confidence. Jake's military haircut and well-groomed beard give him the look of strict discipline.

Wyatt carries the look of a hardcore special operator with his long, shoulder-length hair and full beard. He is intimidating and not the typical FBI agent.

When Wyatt and Jake landed in Missoula, Dan was waiting for them on the tarmac. The first one off the chartered plane was Jake, followed by Wyatt. While shaking Dan's hand, Jake said, "Hey, Boss, good to see you."

Dan nodded and replied, "You too, buddy."

Wyatt said, "Hey, brother, you're looking pretty serious."

Dan smiled and said, "I guess I am Wyatt; we have some pretty badass guys to track down."

"So I've heard. Have you seen the news this morning? It's all over the place about the murders and robberies being tied together."

"That figures. It was just a matter of time," Dan replied. "Maybe we'll get lucky, and these assholes will make a mistake. Let's get your gear loaded up and get to work."

Wyatt said, "How about we stop and pick up something to eat? I'm starving, boss."

Dan laughed and said, "You're always starving. We'll stop on the way to headquarters. I could eat, too."

Pumping his fist, Wyatt said, "Alright! That's what I wanted to hear."

News of the murders in Seattle and Oregon, a leak tying in the robberies, and a Black Charger reached a reporter with Channel 8 news in Seattle. It quickly got plastered over all the major cable news stations.

Tips and sightings of the black Charger have been pouring in from all over Washington State, Oregon, and Idaho. Even some from as far away as Wyoming.

Local city police, Highway Patrol, and County Sheriffs are spread thin following up on the calls.

After Dan, Jake, and Wyatt arrived at Dan's office. Jake commented about all the information covering the walls.

"Looks like you've been pretty busy, Dan."

"This is nothing," Dan shook his head. "There is more coming in from T.J. all the time."

"Good old T.J., he doesn't miss much," Jake replied.

Wyatt said, "I don't know how he does it, I'd go frickin' nuts staring at all that crap, but that's just me. I'd rather be kicking open doors."

Jake replied, "Well, we all have our roles to play, buddy. That one's yours."

Dan sat behind his desk and had just opened his laptop when his phone rang. "Agent Black?"

"Yeah, this is Dan. Go ahead."

"Agent Black, this is Captain Miller with the Missoula County Sheriff's Department. We were told to run all credible leads through you as soon as we got something."

"Yes, that is correct," Dan replied. "What do you have?"

"We've been running down tips all over the County, chasing down Black Chargers since the news hit the airways, but we do have one that sounds pretty solid," said Captain Miller. "Somebody spotted a Black Dodge Charger with two men matching the descriptions of the fugitives. It was sighted in Lolo, Montana. We have two officers watching the house where the Charger is parked, and they confirmed that two men were inside, possibly a third."

Dan replied, "Alright, looks like we maybe caught a break. I don't want anyone to move in or do anything until we get there. We are on our way. Text me the location."

"Sure thing, but it's not an easy place to find. An officer will be waiting for you on the main road in Lolo."

"Sounds good. Just stay out of sight of the house."

"Will do. See you soon."

In Lolo, two County Sheriffs have their trucks pulled down a long gravel driveway leading to the house where the Charger was parked behind a few junk cars and an older Dodge pickup, just outside a steel gate and out of view of the house. Big "No Trespassing" signs are hung on the gate and surrounding fence. The sheriff ran the Montana plates on the pickup but couldn't see the plates on the Charger. The pickup was registered to Mike Wilson, a local resident of Lolo. Wilson showed up with no priors or warrants and is also the homeowner. But the Dodge Charger didn't appear to be owned by Wilson or registered in his name.

On their way to Lolo, Jake told Dan, "I can't imagine these are our guys. I'm pretty sure they aren't stupid enough to be still driving the same car."

"I hear you," Dan replied. "But they were stupid enough to leave all the evidence at the murder scene in Seattle."

Then Wyatt said, "Maybe, just maybe, they screwed up."

"Let's hope so, Wyatt," Jake said doubtfully.

When Dan, Jake, and Wyatt arrived in Lolo, they followed a Country Sheriff and the waiting officers to the driveway, where the officers briefed Dan on the pickup plates and the homeowner.

"Alright, guys, here is what's going to happen. Remember, if these are our guys, they are heavily armed with class three weapons. At least one is a 7.62x51 F.N. SCAR. Remember, your body armor won't stop that round.

"We don't know if these are our guys," he continued, "but we can't take any chances with the possibility of that much firepower. So we are going to move in slowly and quietly. I want Jake and Wyatt to take the lead and get positioned behind cover. I will drive in slowly and make contact with whoever is inside. I want the rest of the officers to follow me in but stay behind for backup.

"I do not want anyone to fire a single shot until I say so. The last thing I want is a shoot-out with some locals thinking we are trespassing. Does everyone understand?"

Wyatt said, "You got it, boss." All the sheriffs nodded in agreement.

"Be careful, Dan," added Jake.

"Alright, Jake, Wyatt, head in. Once you're in position, we'll roll up."

For Jake and Wyatt, this is why they are on Dan's team. They are serious professionals and move with precision and caution into position.

Once Jake and Wyatt gave Dan a signal, a sheriff opened the gate, and Dan drove his SUV fifty yards from the house's front door, followed close behind by three sheriff's trucks.

When Dan stopped, he saw someone pull back a curtain and look out the window. Dan stepped out of the SUV and, over the radio, said, "This is Agent Dan Black of the FBI. I want everyone inside the house to come out slowly with your hands behind your head." It was quiet. Then again, someone peeked out from the window.

Finally, inside the house, someone said. "What the hell is going on? What is this about?"

Dan repeated his demand once again, and once again, it was quiet. Then, finally, Dan got on the radio again and said, "This is Dan Black of the FBI. Come out of the house now!"

Suddenly the front door slowly opened, and out walked Mike Wilson onto the porch with his hands cupped behind his head.

"What the hell is going on?" Wilson asked in a concerned voice.

A sheriff walked up behind Dan and said, "That's Mike Wilson, the owner of this place."

Dan said, "Mr. Wilson, is there anyone else in the house."

Wilson replied, "Yes, my two sons are here visiting from California."

"Mr. Wilson, ask them to come out with you onto the porch."

Two young men walked out of the house and onto the porch. Each held a cell phone in one hand and the other behind their heads. Then, right away, one of them spoke up.

"I'm recording this crap, and you're going to be all over social media."

Wyatt looked over at Jake and said, "Damn cell phones."

Dan asked them to put down the phones and for all three to walk forward.

"No," said one of the young men. "I'm recording this shit."

Mr. Wilson turned to his sons and said, "Put the damn cell phones down and do what he said."

After the three men walked down the porch, Dan, Wyatt, and Jake approached them. Dan explained what was taking place and why they were there. You could tell Mr. Wilson was pissed off but told Dan he had seen everything on the news and understood.

Dan said, "Mr. Wilson, I apologize for the intrusion and what it may have looked like, but we can't take any chances. The fugitives we are after can be holed up anywhere, and we must take every precaution."

Mr. Wilson replied, "I understand, but it looked pretty damn bad seeing you all out here."

Dan reached out and shook Mr. Wilson's hand, "Again, Mr. Wilson, I apologize for the intrusion and inconvenience."

"No problem, Agent. I hope you catch the right guys next time."

"Me too, sir. Have a good rest of your day," Dan replied.

"Agent Black?"

"Yes, sir."

"Don't worry. There won't be any damn video showing up on that Facebook crap. I'll make sure of that."

"Thank you, Mr. Wilson," Dan replied.

Dan, Jake, and Wyatt returned to their SUV and followed the rest of the trucks back into Lolo.

As soon as they got on the Highway, Wyatt said, "Hey, on the way here, I saw a cool-looking burger joint just down the road."

"Really, you're hungry already?" Jake said.

"Hell yeah! When I get excited, I get hungry," he explained.

Dan laughed, "We'll stop and feed the beast, Jake."

"Hell yeah, brother," Wyatt proclaimed. "Feed the beast. I like that."

Jake and Wyatt showed up early at Dan's office the following day. Already at his desk, Dan sat, staring at his laptop. "Morning, guys. Did you get some rest?"

"Sure did," said Jake. "I slept like a rock."

Wyatt yawned and then asked, "Is the coffee fresh?"

"Yeah, you bet. Help yourself, Wyatt. You look like you need it," Dan replied. "By the way, I got a call from Detective Rick Peters from Spokane early this morning. I guess they picked up that service tech who had the security systems down during the robbery at the Casino. He is legit and does work for Valley Security, or at least he did. As soon as they brought him in for questioning, he sang like a bird. It appears that Troy Becker approached him and offered him a deal he couldn't refuse. Being down on his luck, he jumped at a chance to make some easy money. He was given the exact time to have the security system down at the River Bend Casino just before the armored transport arrived.

He had nothing else to give us besides a positive I.D. on Troy Becker.," Dan continued, "He was charged with assisting in a robbery. He'll probably get two years in the state pen."

~ ~ ~

A few hours later, Dan got a call. "Hey, T.J., you got something for me?"

"Yeah, I do. I just sent you all the satellite maps of Blake, Montana, I could find. Unfortunately, they're not current, but they should do."

"Awesome, T.J., I've got Wyatt and Jake here in my office. So we'll take a look."

"What are you thinking, Dan?"

"I don't know," Dan replied. "I have a hunch that's driving me nuts. You say there are a bunch of vacant summer homes up there. Maybe Bishop is holed up in one."

"Yeah, sure are. They're scattered all over the place. It will take days to check them all out, though. Maybe you should do a flyover."

"You know, T.J.," Dan laughed. "Sometimes, I think you can read my mind."

"Hell yeah, I can. I already have a chopper lined up for you and the guys on Saturday."

"Awesome, T.J., What are the details?"

"I'll send you all the information, but it's called West Peak Search and Rescue, based at the Missoula airport. They have a Bell 429 and sound eager to get you guys in the air."

"Thanks, T.J."

"No problem, Dan, You guys be safe."

CHAPTER 15

After packing up camp and loading everything back on top of the Jeep, Sam and John headed down Trapper Creek.

"What a great time, Sam."

"Yep, it sure was. I can't wait to get back up here next weekend."

When they arrived home late that afternoon, Sam pulled the Jeep into the driveway, and the two men started loading all of John's gear back into his truck. Once again, Sam gave John crap about how much gear he'd taken on the trip. "I can't imagine how much stuff you'll bring next weekend."

"It'll be about the same, except more food and my bow."

"Good, If there was going to be any more, I better spend this week building a damn trailer."

John laughed, "Maybe you should. Then we could take the Jeep."

"Yeah, maybe next year."

Sam's wife, Beth, walked outside the house and over to Sam, standing by the Jeep.

"Hey, honey," Beth said. "How was the trip?"

"Hi, sweetheart, It was awesome. We saw a lot of elk and one big bull. I'm going to be hanging one in the house."

Not looking excited, Beth said, "I don't think so. There are too many dang heads on the walls already."

Beth turned to John, "Hi John, did you have a good time?"

"Sure did, It was great. Your husband shamed me into jumping off a cliff into the lake."

"Did you jump too, Sam?"

"Hell yeah, sure did. It was a blast."

Beth shook her head, "You know Sam, you aren't some young kid anymore."

"I'm in my prime," Sam said with a laugh.

"Okay, Doc Holiday," Beth replied. "I've got dinner in the oven. You ready to eat?"

"John, would you like some dinner?"

"Thanks, but I better get home to the wife."

Sam followed John over to his truck and shook his hand.

"I had a great time, buddy."

"We always do, Sam. Take care."

"You too, John. I'll give you a call later in the week."

Sam and Beth stood in the driveway and waved as John drove away. "Well, I hope he makes it home in that Ford."

"Quit it, Sam. Sometimes I wonder how he puts up with you."

"Ahh, He's a great guy. I'm lucky to have him to bum around with."

Beth is six years younger than Sam and is still working as an office manager at the hospital in Kalispell. She grew up in Montana, graduated high school, then attended college at Montana State in Bozeman. Long before meeting Sam, she'd married and moved to North

Carolina. After a divorce, she moved back home to Columbia Falls and went to work at the hospital in Kalispell. When she met Sam, they were a match made in heaven, and after twenty-six years, they both still believed it. She's planning on retiring early and looking forward to taking a trip to Florida with Sam to see where he grew up.

Beth is blonde and very good-looking. Sam jokingly calls her his 'Sugar Mama' and 'Trophy wife.'

~ ~ ~

John's wife, Lisa, was sitting outside by the garden when he pulled up to the house. "Hey honey, I'm home. Aren't you a sight for sore eyes."

"You too, honey. Was it a good trip?"

"It was great, It's beautiful up there, we saw a lot of game."

John walked over to his wife and gave her a kiss and a hug, then placed his hand on her stomach.

"How was your appointment Friday afternoon?"

"I'm due the first week of April."

"Oh my goodness, honey, we're going to have another baby."

With a big smile, Lisa said. "Yes, we are, John."

Lisa and John have wanted to have another baby for quite a while. Lisa had surprised John with the big news on Friday just before leaving on his trip with Sam.

Lisa is in her mid-thirties, slim, with light brown hair. She's been a nurse ever since graduating from college in New Mexico. On her days off, she helps John take care of the farm, but the garden gets most of her attention, along with their five-year-old daughter.

John had taken a few extra days off to spend time with Lisa and his daughter before he and Sam planned to head out on the hunt. It also gives him time to catch up on a few things around the house.

After a few days, Sam called John, inviting him and his family over for a Friday afternoon barbecue. Then they could go over a few final details and catch their wives up on exactly where they will be hunting. Opening day was on Sunday, and they planned on leaving for Trapper Creek early Saturday morning, giving them plenty of time to get things squared away at the cabin and get a good night's sleep before the early hike up the trail.

When John, Lisa, and their daughter arrived at Sam's, Beth greeted them at the front door.

"Come on in, make yourselves at home."

"Congratulations, guys," Beth said, smiling. "Sam said you're expecting another baby."

Lisa placed her hand on her stomach, "Thank you, John and I are pretty excited about it."

"I bet you are."

Even though Lisa had been over a few times, she still couldn't help staring at the walls covered with game and fish mounts.

"Sam's been hunting a long time, hasn't he?"

"Yeah, all his life. He's got this place looking like a wildlife museum." Lisa laughed and walked with Beth into the kitchen.

"Is Sam out back?" John asked Beth.

"Yeah, he's either getting the barbecue ready or in the shop."

When John walked out the back door, Sam was putting ribeye steaks on the grill.

"Hey John, I hope you're hungry."

"You bet. I knew you'd be doing steaks."

"There's beer in the cooler. Help yourself."

After dinner, John told Sam, "Hey, I've got a surprise waiting for you in my truck."

"I already saw you brought all your gear."

"Yeah, that, but walk out there with me."

Sam followed John out to his truck. Then John reached in and pulled out a plastic bag.

"Here you go, buddy."

"What the hell, John, what's this?"

"Just open it up."

Sam opened the bag and inside was a brand-new pair of Vortex Razor 10x42 binoculars.

"What the hell, John, these are for me?"

"Yep., You've been talking about needing new binos, and I figured I'd get you a pair."

"Damn, John, these things are expensive."

"Don't worry about it, buddy."

"Holy crap, thank you, John."

When Sam turned to go into the house to show Beth, she and Lisa were standing on the porch watching the whole exchange.

"Lisa, that sure surprised him," Beth said. "He's been going crazy wanting to get a pair."

"I'm glad, John thinks the world of Sam."

After Sam and John had tossed back a couple more beers, they loaded all of John's gear into Sam's truck, then headed into the backyard by the fire pit and had a few more beers.

"You got a nice place, Sam."

"I like it, but I'm running out of room for all my crap." Sam replied, "I guess we better go in and get the women caught up on where we'll be."

"Sounds good, Sam."

Sam opened up a forest map of the area at the kitchen table. Circled with a red marker was the turn onto Trapper Creek Road, the trailhead, where the cabin was, and a big circle showing where they planned on hunting.

"We won't have cell service up there," Sam said. "But they have a landline at the store in Blake. So if anything changes or we are heading home with an elk, we'll call from there."

"Also, if you need us for anything, send Jason up with this map. Tell him to fire three shots in the air if we aren't at the cabin, and we'll hurry back there to meet him."

Then Sam wrote down Sanders County Sheriff Jim Taylor, "That's the sheriff we told you about. He knows we'll be up there."

Sam paused to ensure he had covered everything, then said, "Well, that's about it. Do you need anything else?"

"No, it looks good, honey. We'll be fine.'

"How about you, Lisa? Got any questions?"

"Nope, Sam, I just want you guys to relax and have a good time. You guys don't have to worry, we'll be okay."

"I know, but just in case, at least you'll know where to find us and how."

Beth walked down to the hall closet and got Sam's digital camera, "Sam, don't forget to take your good camera this time."

"Thanks, honey. I wish I had had it with me when we spotted that bull. I could have got some great pictures."

John walked over and shook Sam's hand, "Well, I guess we better head home. I'll see you at what time?"

Sam laughed and said, "How about five-thirty?"

"Sounds good, buddy. Thanks for the great dinner."

"You bet. Drive safe."

After John walked out to his truck, Lisa looked at Sam, "I thought you weren't going to leave until six-thirty."

Smiling, Sam said, "Well, I figured he'd be late getting here as always."

Lisa laughed. "I'll try to get his butt going early."

Sam laughed, too, "It's no big deal, Lisa. I don't worry about it. Just don't tell him I said that."

"Okay! Sam, please take care of him for me."

Sam gave Lisa a hug, "I'll get him home safe. I promise."

CHAPTER 16

Jack sat in a leather recliner at the log home with his feet up, watching Troy play a first-person shooter video game on the big screen T.V.

"What the hell is it with damn kids and these video games?" asked Jack. "That shit will ruin your mind."

Troy laughed while still glued to the screen. "I know, right?"

Hank finished making three bags of popcorn in the kitchen, which he had brought up from the basement. Then he walked into the living room and plopped down in the recliner next to Jack.

"Here you go, eat up!" Jack grabbed the bowl of popcorn and said nothing. Then, sarcastically, Hank said, "You're welcome."

"Screw off, Hank!"

Hank didn't really know anything about Jack. Jack had approached him in prison about plans to pull off some armed robberies to steal thousands of dollars and said he already had some kid lined up who could get them into Canada. That kid was Troy.

All three men had gotten out of prison around the same time. When they finally met back up on the outside, Jack had shared with them how he wanted things to go down. Troy was to go to Spokane and scope out all the locations. Hank was to secure weapons and ammo. Jack would finish the details and later meet up with them in Spokane.

So far, everything was going as planned, but Hank was getting impatient and kept pushing Jack to get things together. He had no idea he was dealing with someone on the verge of snapping at any moment.

Having finally had enough of the video game Troy was playing, Jack grabbed the remote and scrolled through the channels until he found the news.

The first thing that popped up was the prison mug shots of all three men. Next, the report of the murders in Seattle and Oregon crossed along the bottom of the screen.

"What the hell Jack? Did you really have to kill all three?" Troy said.

Jack just laughed and said nothing.

"Shit, Hank, and you killed the guy in Portland?"

"Yeah, sure did. He was being an asshole and wanted too much for the guns," Hank replied. "So I beat the asshole with a bat." Then he laughed and said, "Good news, all the guns were free."

There was a noticeable shake in Troy's voice when he said, "Jesus Christ, I can't believe it, what the hell. So now we're wanted for murder."

"Quit your damn whining, kid," Jack replied. "If we get caught, I'll tell them you're just a little choir boy."

Then he and Hank laughed as Troy stormed out of the room and went outside. When he was gone, Hank turned to Jack and asked him when he planned to head to Canada.

"Well, thanks to the news, they are getting spread out everywhere looking for us. Especially pretty far south of here. So we'll sit tight here a few more days and get out of here Monday or Tuesday night," Jack said.

Then Hank replied, "About damn time; I'm worried about the kid now."

Jack placed his hand on his knife and said, "Don't worry, we just need him long enough to show us the road into Canada, and then I'll get rid of him."

On the porch of the cabin, Troy paced back and forth, thinking to himself, "*Shit, shit, what in the hell did I get myself into?*"

Then he walked into the garage and over to one of the Razors. He thought to himself, "*he should jump in one and get the hell out of there.*"

But when he walked over and opened the garage door, Jack suddenly entered the garage before Troy could get into the Razor.

"Where do you think you're going, Troy?"

Startled, Troy said, "I was just going to take a ride."

Jack pulled out his knife and walked toward Troy beside the Razor. Troy backed away from Jack as he slammed his blade into both of the Razor's fuel tanks. "Nobody is going anywhere until I say so. Now get your shit together." Then Jack turned and when back inside the cabin.

Shocked, Troy said to himself, "He's frickin' crazy." Then he, too, headed back into the cabin. Hank met him at the door.

"What's up, kid?" Hank asked. "Jack is all pissed off."

Troy looked at Hank and said, "Nothing, it's all good. I'm just ready to get out of here and be done with all this shit."

Shaking his head, Hank said, "Soon enough, kid, just chill the hell out; you're pissing Jack off big time."

~ ~ ~

Late Saturday morning, Hank and Troy leaned against the railing outside on the porch. Then, suddenly, Hank said, "Do you hear that? It's a damn chopper. Go inside and get Jack."

Troy entered the cabin and said, "Hey Jack, you better come out and see this."

Jack walked outside with Troy and stood next to Hank.

"What the hell do you want?" he asked.

Hank pointed up and said, "Don't you hear that? A damn helicopter flew right over us."

Jack looked up and said, "Well did you see it?"

"Just for a minute." Hank replied, "It was blue, and I think I saw '*search and rescue*' on the side of it."

"Well, there you go," Jack said. "That means they probably were coming from some accident. Which way were they heading?"

"They were high and going toward the mountains."

"Don't get freaked out," Jack said. "If they fly over again, let me know. But I bet they don't."

Worried, Troy said, "Maybe we should leave tonight."

Jack glared at him, "I told you, don't worry about it. We are leaving Tuesday." Then Jack went back inside and closed the door.

"What do you think, Hank?" Troy asked.

"He's probably right if we don't hear them again. They're not looking for us."

"I don't like it, Hank."

Hank opened the door and said, "Yeah, so what? Just sit out here and listen. I'm going back inside."

Disgusted, Troy sat on the steps and said aloud, "Goddamn assholes."

After almost an hour, Troy went back into the cabin. Hank and Jack were sitting at the kitchen table. Hank said, "Well, kid, did you hear the chopper again?"

Troy replied, "No, I didn't, but.."

Bishop cut him off and said, "But nothing. Just chill the hell out and shut up about it."

Troy turned and walked out of the kitchen. Under his breath, he said, "asshole," and then he returned to the porch. Troy felt like going and getting in one of the Razors and taking off. But Jack had taken care of that when he stabbed both fuel tanks. Hank had the keys to the truck and never let them out of sight. He thought about talking to Hank about taking the truck and leaving Bishop behind, but then he thought about Hank beating some guy to death with a bat and quickly changed his mind. Once again, Troy thought about how he'd screwed up getting into this mess, and now he was a murder suspect and couldn't afford to get caught.

CHAPTER 17

Early Saturday morning, Sam sat at his dining table, enjoying his third cup of coffee as he looked over hunting area maps on his tablet. As usual, he was up at four a.m. and already had his bow and the rest of his gear loaded in the back of the truck. Beth was still snuggled up in bed, fast asleep. Sam always tried not to wake her but felt she was awake half the time anyways.

At five-thirty, he heard John's truck pull up in front of the house. He double-checked the time on his watch because he couldn't believe John was already there.

Sam went into the bedroom and found Beth just getting out of bed. "Good morning, beautiful."

"Good Morning, Honey," Beth replied. "It sounds like John proved you wrong this morning."

"Yeah, he sure did; I guess I better get going. Do you need anything before I leave?"

Beth smiled at Sam, "I sure do: a big hug and kiss."

Sam walked over to Beth and gave her a hug and a kiss. "I love you, honey."

"I love you too, Sam. Be safe, honey. I want you to come home to me."

Sam hugged Beth again, "I always do, sweetheart. I'll call when I can and check in."

"Okay, Sam. Tell John I said good morning."

"I will, Bye, honey."

"Bye, Sam."

Sam grabbed his go-cup of coffee and headed out the front door.

"Holy crap, redneck, you're actually early," Sam said with amazement.

John laughed. "Yeah, Lisa kicked me out of bed."

"Well, I'll have to thank her when we call later, I'm all loaded up, John. How much you got left?"

"Just a few things," John replied. "I followed your list this time, so I don't think I'm forgetting anything."

"Sounds good, buddy; I think we should stop and get something to eat before we leave town."

"Oh, heck yeah, I'm starving and need more coffee. I'm ready." John said.

Sam and John got in his truck, and as Sam started to drive past the front of the house, he glanced over at the front door and saw Beth waving and blowing him a kiss. Sam blew a kiss back, then drove away.

Then he looked at John and said, "Hey buddy, are you excited?"

"You bet, We've been planning this for a long time."

Sam drove the short distance into town and pulled into the small local restaurant just as they opened their doors.

"Are we going in and sitting down?" John asked.

"Yep, since you showed up early," Sam said. "I feel the need to celebrate. I'm buying."

"Cool beans, buddy."

"Have you and Lisa ever eaten here?" Sam asked.

"No, I don't think so."

"You'd remember," Sam replied. "It's mine and Beth's favorite place for breakfast. Everything on the menu is great. But I'm going for eggs over easy, hash browns, and bacon."

Sam and John were back on the road after a filling breakfast and probably a pot of coffee. They were going to make a lot better time than they had in the Jeep. The trip was quiet, and Sam laughed as he watched John trying to fight off falling asleep.

Finally, on the top of the pass, John was snoring away. Sam slammed on the brakes and yelled, "Oh, shit!!"

John's head slapped up, and his eyes were wide open. "Holy crap, Sam, you scared the shit out of me."

"Sorry buddy, I just couldn't help myself," Sam said, proud of just scaring the hell out of his buddy.

John finally laughed and said, "What an asshole."

Sam grinned and replied, "I know."

"Hey, how about we stop at the store in Blake and see if they have a couple of those deli subs? I should top off the gas anyways."

"Sounds good," John replied.

When they dropped off the pass into the valley floor, the sun shone bright, and the sky was clear blue.

"Damn, this is pretty through here, isn't it?" Sam proclaimed.

"It sure is, It's awesome living in this state," John replied.

Turning the corner and heading into Blake, they saw a county sheriff's truck parked at the store.

"Hey, I wonder if that's our buddy?" John asked.

Sam replied, "I bet it is."

When Sam pulled up to the gas pumps, Sheriff Jim Taylor exited the store. "Hey, Sheriff, fancy seeing you here," Sam said.

"Hey guys, you headed back up to the cabin?" The officer asked.

"Yep, opening day is tomorrow, and I have a date with a bull elk," Sam replied with a big smile.

"Wow! That sounds good," Sheriff Taylor replied. "The weather is going to cool off starting tomorrow and should help get the elk bugling."

"I hope so, Jim," John said. "We're going to be up there all week. If you feel like it, driving up."

"I don't know, guys, It's one crappy road, but we'll see. Take care, guys, and be safe." Sheriff Taylor replied.

"Thanks, officer. Hope you have a good day." Sam replied.

Sheriff Taylor got in his truck and headed north toward the mountain pass.

Sam finished filling up his truck, and he and John went into the store to check out the sub sandwiches. The clerk immediately recognized John and was quick to say hello. Then he walked out from behind the counter to shake John's hand.

"I'm Randy, I guess I didn't get a chance to introduce myself last time you were here. Are you heading back up Trapper Creek?" the clerk asked.

"We are, I'm John, and this is my hunting buddy Sam."

Sam shook the clerk's hand and said, "It's a pleasure to meet you. We plan to stay at the cabin all week, maybe longer."

Then John said, "Unless we get lucky and get our elk early."

"Well, guys, you know it's getting hot in the afternoons." Randy said, "What are you going to do with the meat?"

Sam said, "After we pack it out, we plan on taking it home."

"No need for all that," Randy replied, "I've got a big walk-in freezer in the back, and you would be more than welcome to store your meat in there if you need to."

John excitedly said, "Really! What would you charge us?"

"Nothing, John. I really appreciate how you stepped in and helped me out the other day. It's the least I can do."

"Sounds great!" Sam said, "I hope we can take you up on that offer."

Sam and John picked out a couple of subs and a few snacks, then paid at the counter. Sam shook Randy's hand again and said, "Thanks again for the offer. We may be taking you up on it."

"No problem. You guys be safe and good luck on your hunt." Randy said.

After Sam and John left the store and headed south toward Trapper Creek, John said. "That's pretty awesome of him to offer to let us use his freezer."

"Yeah, we lucked out there." Sam said, "That's the only part of this hunt I was worried about. We'll have it made as long as we can get the meat packed out fast enough."

CHAPTER 18

Dan, Jake, and Wyatt looked over the maps that T.J. had sent over. As T.J. had said, the homes were spread out up and down the valley. From what they could see, some were pretty remote and hidden in thick timber, making it difficult to make out in the satellite images. The area was a maze of roads and long driveways.

Wyatt said, "Damn, it will take days to cover all that area."

Jake shook his head. "We're going to need a lot more people, Dan."

Looking hard at the maps, Dan said, "Well, guys, unfortunately, we will be on our own. Local County Sheriff departments are spread too thin as it is. So trying to get them to assist in a house-to-house search isn't going to happen, and honestly, they aren't really on board with my hunch."

"Well, that's great," said Jake sarcastically. "We'll have no help at all?"

"We have one guy that will join us when we hit the ground up there: Officer Jim Taylor from the Sanders County Sheriff's Department," replied Dan, "He's been patrolling the area around Blake and volunteered to help out the best he can."

"Sounds good," Wyatt chuckled. "At least we have a tour guide."

~ ~ ~

Dan, Jake, and Wyatt pulled up to the West Peak Search and Rescue gate early Saturday morning in their black SUV. Dan pressed the speaker button on the keypad. A voice came over the speaker. "Good morning, Agent Black?"

"Yes, sir, it is."

The chain link gate opened, and Dan pulled the SUV to the office. Meeting them at the door was Don West. An older man, perhaps in his early to mid-seventies, Don wore a leather flight jacket that looked like it was from the Vietnam War and was covered with medevac flight patches.

Reaching out and shaking Dan's hand, Don said, "Good morning, gentleman. I'm Don West, the owner. Please come on in."

"Pleasure to meet you, Don. I'm Dan. I spoke to you on the phone. These are my colleagues, Jake and Wyatt," Dan said.

Don shook their hands and said, "I've got some fresh coffee and a box of donuts inside if you care for any."

Wyatt quickly replied, "Heck yeah, donuts and coffee sound great."

The four men entered the office, helped themselves with the coffee and donuts, then sat at a long table. Wyatt couldn't help but notice Don's hand shaking while he raised his cup to take a sip. Wyatt didn't want to be rude, but he had to ask. "Are you our pilot?"

Don laughed and said, "Oh, hell no, I'm retired, and my desk is the only thing I fly anymore. However, I have two very experienced pilots that work for me, and yours should be here any minute now." Wyatt gave a slight sigh of relief but made sure Don didn't notice.

Don opened up his file cabinet and took out a folder. "I spoke to Agent Tanner Jones from Seattle yesterday. He sent over some information to me. A lot of information."

Dan smiled and said, "That's T.J. for you. He's pretty thorough about details."

Nodding, Don said, "When Myles gets here, he'll review the flight plans and the standard safety stuff with you guys. You probably have plenty of experience, but it's standard procedure."

Dan replied, "No problem."

"Another thing," added Don, "While you're in the air, if we get a call for an emergency, your flight will be cut short."

Dan said, "Certainly, we understand." Wyatt and Jake both agreed.

After several more minutes, Myles pulled through the gate and up to the office. Don said, "There's your pilot now."

Myles walked into the office and, after a round of introductions, poured himself a cup of coffee, grabbed a couple of donuts, and sat down at the table.

"I understand I'll be taking you up around the Blake area this morning."

Dan told Myles he was interested in flying over the area to get an idea of what it looked like and see what it would take to do a ground search of the homes in the valley.

Myles said. "I'm real familiar with the area and the Cabinet mountains. We get quite a few rescue calls in the mountains up there every year. From lost hikers and hunters, it can be a busy area. Opening day archery season opens tomorrow, so I expect we'll see smoke from campfires in the mountains and lower in the valley."

Myles laid a map on the table and reviewed the areas Dan wanted to fly over. Then he explained the flight plan in detail to the three agents. Then after quickly going over the standard safety guidelines, Myles told Dan he could follow him in the SUV around the hanger. Wyatt and Jake followed Don down the hallway to the hangar. Inside the hangar sat a blue Bell 429 helicopter.

"Wow, that is one good-looking chopper," Jake said surprisedly.

"Yeah, it's my pride and joy," Don beamed. "We take good care of that one."

He then pressed the button that opened the hangar doors. Then Don motioned to Dan to pull the SUV into the hangar next to the helicopter. "You guys can unload your gear, and we'll get this show on the road."

Wyatt and Jake unloaded the gear from the back of the SUV onto the hangar floor, and then Dan pulled it back around to the office. Next, Myles started doing some of his pre-flight checks. After Don had helped Wyatt and Jake load their gear into the storage compartments, Myles instructed Wyatt and Jake to help roll the Bell 429 out of the hangar. Once clear of the hangar and the other three men clear of the helicopter, Myles finished the pre-flight check and started the twin turboshaft engines.

Don shook all three men's hands and told them to have a good flight. Then Dan took the front seat next to Myles, while Jake and Wyatt took their seats in the back. Myles pointed to the headsets, and after the three men had them on, Myles asked if they could hear him.

"Yes, loud and clear," they replied, giving Myles the thumbs up. Then, over the radio, Myles communicated to the tower that he was ready for take-off and verified his flight plan. Once Air Traffic Control had given them clearance, Myles checked again with Dan, Wyatt, and Jake.

"Okay, guys, is everyone buckled in and ready to go?" All three men gave another thumbs up.

"Alright, here we go."

The lift-off was smooth as the 429 cleared the tops of the nearby hangars, then headed northwest over the city and the interstate highway. The skies were clear blue, and once the helicopter reached twelve thousand feet and a cruising speed of one hundred and thirty miles per hour, the view was nothing less than spectacular. In the distance, the three agents could already see the tall, majestic peaks of the Cabinet wilderness. Below them was a thick pine forest that only opened its canopy to an occasional home. Their flight path followed along a beautiful river, and Dan, Wyatt, and Jake forgot what they were there to do for a while. Wyatt thought how amazing it would be to float the river with his fly rod and how peaceful it would be.

Over the radio, Myles said, "Alright, guys, soon we'll see the highway heading north to Blake. I have a range of about three hundred miles. But I've made arrangements at a small airport in Libby to refuel if necessary."

"Sounds great, Myles. This is some amazing country," Dan replied.

"You haven't seen anything yet. We'll be getting real close to the peaks you see to the north."

Myles turned north once he hit the highway and slowed to one hundred miles per hour. Below them was another small river, and forest roads winding through the trees. Thirty miles from Blake, they spotted the first home. Then more and more vacant homes were scattered along the river and onto the foothills on both sides of the highway. Small ranches with open meadows dotted the countryside.

"Alright, guys, we have the sky to ourselves," Myles said. "Let me know if you want to take a better look somewhere."

"Alright, Myles, thanks," Dan replied. "Do you have any idea how many people live up here year-round?"

"Not many, Dan. Winter is tough up here. Really, only a handful, mainly in or close to the small town of Blake."

Scattered few and far between, they could see small traces of smoke rising from the forest and higher up on the foothills of the Cabinet mountains. Jake said, "That must be campfires from hunters, right, Myles?"

"Yeah, most likely, or maybe some die-hard hikers heading into the wilderness. It's beautiful this time of the year. So, what exactly do you want to see?"

Dan said on the radio, "I'm mainly wanting to get a lay of the land and see what we'll be getting ourselves into if we come back."

"Yeah," said Wyatt, "If we see three guys standing by a black Dodge Charger and waving at us, that will work too."

Dan and Jake chuckled, then Jake said, "Yeah, we can only hope they would be that damn stupid."

Soon the helicopter passed over Blake and circled back to the east, closer to the mountains heading back to the south. Below them, the men could see the long driveways to vacant homes and some disappearing into the timber. After a few more miles, Myles turned to the west, then north along the foothills on the other side of the river. Again, it was the same thing, driveways to vacant homes and an occasional forest or gated logging road.

On the radio, Myles said, "Well, guys, that's about it. We can head north about ten miles further, but there aren't any more homes until you get close to Libby. So if you want to stay airborne longer, we'll have to refuel to Libby."

Dan said. "No, that's fine. I've seen what I wanted. So we can head back."

"How would you feel about flying over the wilderness and taking in some amazing views of Montana?" Myles asked.

Wyatt immediately chimed in and said. "Hell yeah, brother! What do you think, Dan?"

Dan nodded his head and said, "Sounds good. Why not?"

Wyatt excitedly pumped his fist and let out a big "wo-hoo!"

Jake rubbed his head and said, "Wyatt, "Sometimes, I think you're just a kid." All four men laughed as the Bell 429 turned southeast and climbed to fifteen thousand feet.

The Cabinet wilderness is over ninety thousand acres running north to south. The line of snow-capped peaks rises to over eight thousand feet. The tallest is Snowshoe Peak at eight thousand seven hundred feet. It is spectacular. From the air, the men could see the high alpine meadows and the deep blue lakes hiding between the peaks and valleys. Large groves of giant western red cedars cover the canopied valleys. The large rock formations and long mountain slopes are home to Mountain Goat and Bighorn Sheep. The thickly timbered valleys and open meadows are home to large numbers of elk and deer. Grizzly bears roam the huge berry thickets of huckleberries, thistleberries, and wild blackberries.

When Myles flew over the lower portion of the wilderness, Jake spotted small streams of smoke rising from the valley floor.

"Is that all hunt camps, Myles?" Jake asked over his headset.

"Yeah, It's outfitter camps. Archery season opens tomorrow, remember?"

Then Wyatt spotted three wall tents in an open meadow next to a slow-moving stream. "Wow! What a camp," he exclaimed.

Then they saw five people waving at the helicopter as they flew over the camp. Wyatt said, "Damn, they have it made. I wish I were there, I'll have to check it out someday."

Myles replied, "Yeah, it would be nice. If you have an extra ten thousand bucks lying around."

Shocked, Wyatt said, "Ten thousand bucks. Are you kidding me?"

"Nope, outfitting is big business," Myles said. "A lot of people pay big money for the chance to hunt with a guide for trophy elk and sheep."

"Holy crap, I guess I need a raise, Dan." Wyatt proclaimed. Dan laughed.

"I'll see what I can do." Dan said with a chuckle, "I'm sure the Bureau would be happy to pay you more."

Wyatt just snickered, "Yeah, right. I'm sure."

After being cleared by Air Traffic Control, Myles touched down in Missoula. Don West greeted the three agents back at the hanger. "How was the flight, guys?"

Dan replied, "It was great, Don, very helpful. We got a good idea of the area near Blake."

Nodding his head, Don said, "That's good. I'm glad we could help out."

That country is impressive," Jake proclaimed. "Hard to imagine just how vast it is."

Wyatt chimed in, "Yeah, someone could get lost for years in that country."

"Believe it or not, some have," Don replied, "Well, if one of you wants to give Myles a hand, you can take all your gear to your rig."

"I got it," Jake volunteered.

Dan and Wyatt followed Don through the hallway and back to his office. Don shook Wyatt's and Dan's hands. "Well, gentlemen, call us if you need us again."

"Will do. Thank you for everything," Dan replied.

Jake was out front with Myles and had just finished loading the gear back into the SUV. Then walked into the office and told Dan, "Everything is loaded up, boss." Then he thanked Don, and the three agents walked to the SUV. Dan thanked Myles and shook his hand. Wyatt and Jake did the same. Then they piled into the SUV and left for Dan's office back at the field office.

Dan was quiet the entire way back to the office. Once they arrived, Jake asked, "What were you thinking about, boss?"

Dan paused, rubbed his neck, and said, "I don't know, guys. There's just too much for us to cover by ourselves. Especially just going on a hunch."

Jake said, "Don't start second-guessing yourself; your hunches are usually right."

"Yeah, I agree," said Wyatt. "We've followed your hunch before, and they usually pay off. So I'm all in, boss."

Dan said, "Thanks, guys. We'll have to focus on that area come Monday unless we catch a break before then. I need to give T.J. a call when we get to the office."

~ ~ ~

Dan sat at his desk in the office and quickly booted up his laptop. Jake and Wyatt sat down and could tell Dan was all business.

Jake asked, "Are you good, boss?"

Dan reached over to the phone on the desk and dialed T.J.

"I'm good, guys. I want to get these guys."

When T.J. answered, Dan said, "T.J., I've got you on speaker. Jake and Wyatt are with me."

"Hi, Dan. Jake, Wyatt."

"Hey, T.J., how's my favorite desk jockey?" Wyatt asked jokingly.

T.J. laughed. "I'm doing good. What's up, guys? How was the flight?"

"It was good, T.J.," Dan replied. "That country up around Blake is huge. I don't know how we'll cover it all."

"You'll figure it out, Dan. I was thinking about your hunch and wanted to know if you'll go with it. If so, you should get some rooms in Libby. It will be much closer, and you won't have to drive back and forth from Missoula."

Dan said, "That sounds good, T.J. Can you find us three rooms at a motel up there?"

"I'm way ahead of you again, Dan. I've got three rooms on hold at a lodge outside Libby. Plus, it's on its way to Blake. So I just need to know when you're going, and I can leave the rooms open-ended."

"You're the best T.J."

"I do what I can, boss. Also, I've got the Sanders County Sheriff's Department on board. They agreed to have Officer Jim Taylor team up with you for as long as it takes."

"That's great news, T.J., I was planning on heading that way Monday, but I want to get settled in tomorrow."

"Alright, Dan, I'll make the calls and send you the information asap," T.J. assured Dan. "Oh, while I've got you on the phone, I've done some more digging into the fugitive's backgrounds. I found Troy Becker's old high school buddy from when he lived in Eureka, Montana.

They were close and bounced around the same foster homes. The guy is in Libby, and I had the local police pick him up for questioning. He checked out but did have some pretty interesting information.

"It sounds like when he and Troy were on the run from local police for petty misdemeanors," T.J. continued, "they would take ATVs on an old gravel back road to the Canadian border."

"I knew it, T.J." Dan slapped his desk and grinned. "That's got to be why Bishop recruited him. So that's where they are going. What about the border patrol up there?"

"Bad news about that, Dan," T.J. said. "Check stations are on each side of the border, but neither is operated full-time. So instead, once a week, a U.S. Border Agent drives up there and spends just a few days.

Jake said, "Jesus, that figures. They could be long gone by now, and we'll be left chasing our tails."

T.J. said, "That could be Jake, I've been in touch with U.S. and Canadian border patrol. They assured me they have agents up there now. Let's hope Bishop and his crew are still in the area."

"Great job, T.J.," Dan said. "Anything else?"

"That's it for now, Dan. I'll get those rooms for you."

"Thanks, T.J., we'll be knocking on a few doors.

"Sounds good, Dan. At least you have two of the best door kickers with you."

Wyatt laughed and said, "Thanks, T.J. Later, buddy."

Then Dan ended the call and told Jake and Wyatt to prepare everything to leave early in the morning.

CHAPTER 19

The twenty miles to the turnoff to Trapper Creek took little time, and soon Sam turned onto the rough mountain road. "Well, John, eight miles of badass road to the cabin, it's going to suck in this three-quarter ton."

John replied, "Boy, I guess, slow and steady, buddy."

Sam's three-quarter-ton Chevy pickup suspension is heavy and stiff. Definitely not built for rough, rocky forest roads. Especially roads like Trapper Creek.

Sam took his time as he drove up the switchbacks, trying to avoid some of the biggest rocks and washouts. Still, John and Sam moaned each time the heavy truck bounced over a big rock, or one of the tires dropped into a washout.

While holding onto the grab handle above his head, John said, "Damn, I knew this would be bad, but this sucks."

Sam laughed and said, "Yeah, I'm going to have to build a trailer to pull behind the Jeep. I should get it done this summer."

"I'll help you build one this winter, buddy, "John chuckled. "Don't want you to get all lazy over the winter."

"Sounds like a plan, John."

When Sam and John finally caught a glimpse of the roof of the cabin, Sam said, "There it is, home sweet home."

"Hey Sam, this might be the wrong time to ask, but did you remember to get the combination for the lock?" John said.

"Sure did, the Forest Service emailed me the combination."

When they pulled up to the cabin, Sam and John jumped out of the truck, and both men stretched their backs. Sam said, "Thank God we made it. That was one rough-ass trip."

"Boy, I guess." John replied, "Hopefully, the trip down will be with a monster bull. I hope this is the year."

Sam walked over to the truck's passenger side and, grabbed a piece of paper from the glove box, then walked over to the lock on the cabin door. The heavy cabin door creaked open. "Damn, we need to sweep this place out and check for spiders."

John laughed, "Oh yeah, I forgot you're scared of spiders."

"Hell yeah, I'm not scared of much, but those things creep my ass out," Sam said.

Laughing again, John said. "Don't worry, buddy, I'll protect you."

Sam smiled and said, "Thanks, hillbilly."

Luckily, a broom and dustpan were sitting in the corner of the cabin. "Do you want to sweep or start unloading the truck, Sam?"

Thinking about spiders, Sam quickly said, "I'll start unloading. You can sweep."

"You got it."

It wasn't long before John had the cabin swept out and was able to help Sam finish unloading the truck. Then they started unpacking all their gear and organizing everything in the cabin. Sleeping pads were laid out on the beds, and when John pulled out his sleeping bag, Sam immediately said, "Holy shit, you got a new bag."

"Sure did," John replied. "I told Lisa about the crap you gave me the last time, and she brought me a new sleeping bag home."

"Well, she's a good lady, John."

John walked out onto the small porch and said, "I guess I should get some firewood cut and ready to go."

"Hang on a minute. Let's take the truck down to where we camped. There's still a shitload all stacked up from last time."

Sam and John drove the short distance to the stacks of firewood and loaded it all up in the back of the truck. When they were ready to take it back to the cabin, they both heard a helicopter down toward the valley.

"I wonder what that's about?" said John.

Sam replied, "Who knows? Just hope they don't fly around and spook the elk."

"No shit, wouldn't that suck, "John said. "But it sounds like it's a long ways from us."

Sam and John unloaded the wood at the cabin and stacked it along its porch. Sam surveyed the stack and said, "I think we have more than enough wood to last the whole trip. We really aren't going to need much."

"It's going to get into the middle sixties during the day and only drop down in the low forties at night."

John said, "Yeah, I wish it would get colder like we first thought. But at least we'll have some nice campfires to sit around at night."

Sam said, "Maybe a cold front will roll in."

"Oh yeah, what do you think about doing a spike camp up on top if we run into elk late and can't make a stalk?"

"I'm down with that, Sam. Did you bring a tent or a tarp?"

Sam smiled and said, "Of course I did. I've got both. I never forget stuff."

John laughed and said, "Oh yeah, what about last year? First, we drive all the way to Miller Lake to camp and fish. Then when we get ready to paddle out with the pontoon boats, you forgot to bring paddles."

"Well, you got me there," Sam said. "Damn, I was pissed off at myself. When I raced home to get them, I think I cussed all the way."

John laughed. "I bet you did."

"Then, when I got home, Beth sure gave me some crap."

John smiled and said, "I'm sure she did."

"You know, buddy, what was cool about it, though? When I got back late to camp, you had a hot dinner waiting for me," Sam said.

John replied, "That's no big deal, Sam."

"It is to me, John."

John smiled. "Well, the worst part of the story was that we fished for two days and didn't catch a single fish. It was too dang hot."

~ ~ ~

Sam and John went into the cabin, started packing their backpacks, and laid out all the gear they planned to take on the hunt the following day.

Both packs were jammed full of gear. Each pack contained four game bags, food, snacks, and all the necessary survival gear. Sam laid out his new binoculars, and John strapped the spotting scope and tripod to the side of his pack. In Sam's pack was his camera that Beth reminded him to take. They both tied their elk bugles to the side of their packs, then double-checked to ensure they had their diaphragm calls.

Sam and John had practiced for months with the calls, imitating the bugles and grunts made by bull elk. They also practiced cow and calf calls that can sometimes bring a wary bull within bow range.

Sam had bugled in elk before, but it would be the first time for John to try. When he first got his calls, Sam gave John a lot of crap about his bugling. Sam said he sounded like a wounded chipmunk. But now John had all the calls down to perfection and was confident he could entice a leery bull into Sam's setup.

Bugling in a bull elk close enough to make a clean, humane shot with a bow is, without a doubt, one of the most exciting and rewarding hunts you can ever be on. You never know how the bull you're hunting is going to react. He can come in on the first bugle, in full charge, ready to fight to defend his harem of cows. Next time a bull can come in slow and cautious, using every sense at his disposal. Their incredible eyesight can pinpoint precisely where a sound is coming from over a hundred yards away. Any movement will stop them in their tracks. With excellent hearing, they can hear a single twig snap at two hundred yards. But their most used defense is their sense of smell, one thousand times more acute than that of humans. Even the slightest change in wind direction will send a bull into the next county.

To be successful, your preparation and knowledge are crucial, but with so much stacked against you, luck has to be on your side as well.

~ ~ ~

That evening, Sam and John relaxed by the light of a warm fire. The time had come, and for a while, they sat quietly, thinking to themselves about what had got them to this point and how fortunate they were to be there at that moment in time.

Sam looked over at John and saw him looking intensely into the fire. "What are you thinking about, John?"

John looked up from the fire and said, "Everything, Sam. I'm so excited to be up here hunting with you."

"Same here, buddy," Sam said. "I'm glad you're here. Tomorrow is a big day."

Sam reached down, put another piece of wood on the fire, and then poked at the coals with a stick. "Wouldn't it be awesome to get a big bull tomorrow?"

"That would be sweet. I hope so, Sam."

Then Sam and John started going over all kinds of scenarios and fantasizing about different stories of how the hunt would go. Each one ended up with the massive herd bull piled up on the ground.

The night cooled, and stars lit up the sky. The crackling of the fire was interrupted only by the laughter of the two friends.

Soon Sam said, "Well, I guess I'm going to turn in. We'll be getting up early."

"Me too. This has been great," John replied.

Sam went into the cabin while John took a stick and spread the hot coals around in the fire pit. Then he, too, went into the cabin and went to sleep.

CHAPTER 20

S am was up early Sunday morning, and the long-anticipated opening day of the hunt was finally upon them.

The clear, cool night sky had brought a chill to the inside of the cabin. After getting out of his sleeping bag, Sam found his headlamp lying on his backpack beside his bunk. Then he gathered some kindling from the wood box next to the stove. It was only a short time before he had a fire in the small wood stove. The chill in the air quickly left the small cabin. Sam sat on the edge of his bunk, fumbled in his pack, and finally pulled a knife from one of the side punches. It was a custom, handmade skinning knife he'd made for John.

The handle was made from a beautiful piece of elk antler. The blade was hand-forged from a raw billet of A2 steel, heat treated and tempered in Sam's shop, with a razor-sharp edge that had been hand-polished to a mirror finish. Finally, it was wrapped in a custom leather sheath with a bear claw etched into the dark leather.

Sam had worked on the blade off and on all summer. He has handmade hundreds of knives since he retired. He gave all his family members what to him were art pieces and sold over a hundred to customers wanting a true custom knife. But Sam believed this knife was the best he had ever made and was a gift to his good friend.

John was still sleeping while Sam finished getting dressed in his camouflage hunting clothes and laced up his boots. Then Sam left the cabin to start a fire to get the coffee brewing. But before he did, he laid the knife on John's backpack. Sam made sure the cabin door squeaked when he opened it, but John didn't hear a thing. Sam laughed and shook his head, thinking to himself, "How in the hell can he sleep so hard? I guess I'll wake him when coffee is ready."

Sam sat in a camp chair beside the fire with a cup of coffee, looking up at the thousands of stars lighting up the sky. Then, quietly to himself, he said a prayer of thankfulness for the opportunities God had set before him.

Soon he heard John rustling around in the cabin like a bear. Then Sam heard John say, "What the hell?"

When the cabin door opened, John walked out onto the porch. Sam looked at him and thought to himself, *what a sight.*

John stood there with a big smile, wearing his sleeping pants tucked into his unlaced boots, a tattered long-john shirt, and his ball cap cocked to the side of his head.

"Good morning, buddy," Sam said.

"Good morning, Sam, What is this?" John said, holding up the knife.

"It's yours, buddy."

"Holy crap, this thing is beautiful. You didn't have to make me a knife."

"I know I didn't. Coffee's ready."

John walked over and sat down, and Sam poured him a cup of coffee. John sipped the coffee and asked, "What time is it, anyway?"

"It's early, Four o'clock, probably," Sam said. "So we've got time to relax and eat breakfast."

John looked at the knife and said, "I can't believe it. I love it."

"I'm glad. I hope you get to use it today." Sam replied.

Then John asked, "Why don't you carry any of your knives?"

Sam took his knife out of its sheath and handed it to John, then Sam said, "That's the only hunting knife I've ever used. My mom got it for me when I was eight years old. In my pack is the buck-skinning knife Beth got for me twenty years ago."

John handed the knife back to Sam. "Damn, that thing is fifty-eight years old."

Sam smiled, "I suppose it is."

John returned to the cabin and started getting his hunting clothes on, and Sam started on breakfast.

From the cabin, John asked, "What's for breakfast?"

"Well, I figured I'll make eggs, sausage, and hash browns."

"Cool beans, buddy. What can I do?"

"Nothing, but if you want, you can grab my pack and get our bows out of the truck."

"You bet, Sam."

"Oh yeah, and grab my watch. It's on the table."

Sam settled in next to the campfire, cooking breakfast, then suddenly heard John say, "Dang, it's just now four o'clock" Sam chuckled and continued cooking. When John rejoined Sam by the fire, he handed Sam his watch.

Then John said, "Well, I guess we're getting an early enough start."

Sam replied, "Yeah, maybe we can get to where we saw the elk before it gets hot, and they are still roaming around."

After breakfast, Sam and John strapped their backpacks to the pack frames they would use to pack out the elk, and then they strapped their bows onto the backpacks. Finally, Sam extinguished the fire, and both men helped each other with their packs.

Sam's pack was forty pounds and plenty heavy, especially with his bow strapped on the back. When Sam picked up John's pack, he said, "Holy crap, what do you have in here, rocks?"

John laughed. "Not much. Cokes for you."

Sam laughed, and the two men left for the trailhead.

Sam led the way as they began the long climb up the switchbacks. They were lucky it was a clear sky, and the light from the almost-full moon lit up the trail. Their headlamps helped as they climbed over the deadfall across the trail and other obstacles along the way. Even with their heavy packs, they were making good time.

Trying to be as quiet as possible, both men thought about surprising a grizzly that could be sharing the same trail.

Both men had their forty-forty magnums and the retaining straps that secured them in the holsters hanging loose in case they had to draw them quickly.

Sam often stopped to catch his breath and adjust his pack. John was glad he did but was always amazed at the pace his sixty-six-year-old friend could set.

At almost every corner, they expected to run into something. Both men jumped and reached for their handguns when two mule deer busted out across the trail just a few feet in front of them.

"Damn, that scared the shit out of me," John said.

In a whisper, Sam said, "Me too. You can't see much in the timber."

Even with the bright moonlight, the thick timber was still dark, making it hard to see anything more than ten yards away.

The early start was paying off, and it was just getting light by the time they reached the trail to Lost Lake. Sam found a place to sit down and slid his pack off his shoulders. John did the same, and both men sat on the side of the trail.

"Time for a snack, Sam?"

Sam said, "Oh yeah, we've earned it."

After his snack and drink, Sam reached into his pocket, grabbed his elk call, and took his grunt tube off his pack.

"Time to give a shout-out," Sam said. Then he took a deep breath and gave out a long bugle, followed by several grunts.

Then both men were completely quiet. Nothing, it was dead silent. Sam sat back down, and they just sat there listening. Then, suddenly, way off in the distance, they heard their answer. A bull broke his silence and gave away his position.

He was a long way off, but he was willing to talk. Sam didn't call again. Instead, they got to their feet and unstrapped their bows from their packs, then helped each other put their packs back on and continued up the trail, stopping at every opening in the canopy to glass with their binoculars.

Sam checked the wind with his puffer over and over again. The wind was swirling but wasn't against their backs.

By the time they reached the ridgeline that overlooked the creek and valley where they had spotted the huge herd bull, the sun had risen over the tall peaks to the east. It was warming up quickly and was going to get hot.

Sam walked off the trail to the spot they found during their scouting trip, and John followed. They dropped their heavy packs and stripped down to their lightweight shirts. Sam took out a bottle of scent blocker, and both men sprayed each other down. Then they strapped their chest holsters back on and their chest rigs for their binoculars. John unpacked the spotting scope and tripod from his pack and the smaller day pack, which was the perfect size to carry the spotting scope and tripod. Then they followed the trail and moved slowly down the ridge. Sam spotted movement in the timber on the second ridge. They were only two hundred yards away from their packs and already spotted elk moving slowly through the trees. The elk were over a thousand yards away and hard to see.

Sam whispered to John, "We should get a little higher above the trail." John agreed, and they quietly eased off the trail and found a perfect place to glass the elk. There was plenty of cover, and they dug in behind a big pine blowdown. Sam glassed with his binoculars and spotted a bull.

"There's a bull," he whispered in an excited voice.

John glassed but didn't see the bull. "Is it the big guy?"

"No, but it looks like it could be the six-point we saw," Sam replied. "He's hard to see. He's bedded down close to those two cows."

John hurried to set up the spotting scope, then quickly zoomed in and found the bull. "Sam, I think that is the same six-point," John said. Then Sam eased over to the spotting scope to take a look.

Excited, Sam said, "I think you're right. That's got to be him. The bigger bull is there somewhere."

Suddenly a loud, deep bugle ripped across the valley. "Holy shit, that's him," Sam said while shaking his fist.

"What now, Sam? Are you going to bugle back?"

"No, we need to watch them for a while. It looks like they are all going to bed down. We have to be patient and not blow it." Sam said.

John whispered, "Sounds good, buddy. How dang exciting is this."

Sam glanced over at John and said, "It's awesome."

Both men got quiet and made little movement. Sam's eyes stayed glued to the binoculars.

At least an hour passed, during which time Sam spotted four more cows in the timber. The day was getting warm, and John was fighting to keep his eyes open. Each time his head would bob, he'd snap it back up. Then, suddenly, he spotted antlers coming up the ridge back down the trail right across from where they had dropped their packs.

John reached over, tapped Sam on his back, and pointed down the trail. Sam turned slowly just in time to see a raghorn bull crest the ridge and walk onto the trail. Just behind him, a spike followed close behind.

Both men slowly notched an arrow in their bows as the elk walked down the trail toward them. Sam and John were set up only thirty yards above the trail. The raghorn and his young companion had no idea they were there.

In his mind, Sam fantasized about the big herd bull appearing next and walking down the trail. Sam and John sat motionless as the two young bulls walked past them, only twenty-five yards away.

For most hunters, the hunt would be over, and the raghorn bull would have been dropped in its tracks. But there was a bigger bull one thousand yards away, plus the possibility of the big herd bull that bugled earlier.

Sam and John patiently watched the elk drop back down into the small valley and vanish. Finally, John whispered, "Damn, that was intense." Sam nodded and got back to glassing.

Sam felt guilty because he had a good idea that John would have happily taken the raghorn. He hoped he wouldn't regret it.

After another thirty minutes, the six-point bull got up out of his bed and shook his rack. Then he gave out a high-pitch bugle. Momentarily, a low, raspy bugle echoed across the valley. Finally, the huge herd bull materialized out of nowhere one hundred yards above the six-point. Sam was ready to move and pointed out to John where they needed to go to circle above the elk.

John nodded, and both men stood up. They moved up higher and started to slowly sidehill toward the far ridge just above the bulls.

Sam stopped and whispered to John, "If you have a shot on either of the bulls, you take it." John shook his head no.

Then whispered to Sam, "It's your shot, Buddy."

"You better take it if you got it," Sam insisted, then moved farther through the timber.

When Sam stopped to check the wind, his heart dropped. The wind had changed direction, and if they went any further, they would be busted, and the elk would clear the area. It would only take the slightest whiff, and it would all be over. Sam pointed at his puffer, squeezed it, then motioned for John to backtrack.

Once they returned to where they'd been. Sam glassed over to the elk. They were still there, and the big bull stood in the open.

Both men sat down, and Sam told John the wind was going to bust them, and they couldn't chance getting any closer.

"What about calling him in?" John suggested.

Sam said, "I don't know, it's too risky. That big bull is smart and pretty damn cautious. I think the only way we'll get a shot at him is if we cut him off." John agreed, and the two men moved back to where they'd dropped their packs.

John asked, "What now, buddy."

"We hike back farther down the trail and have lunch and keep an eye on the wind," Sam replied.

"Sounds good to me, Sam."

Sam and John put on their packs and hiked back down the trail several hundred yards from where they'd first spotted the elk, then sat down and dug their lunches out of their packs. John wasn't kidding when he said he was packing Cokes.

"Thank you, buddy."

Then John asked, "How can you be so calm about seeing the elk? I'm going nuts!"

Sam laughed. "Believe me. I'm not. That six-point is one hell of a trophy, but the seven-point is the biggest bull I've ever seen during hunting season. He's Pope and Young, for sure. I bet he's in the top ten easily. We've got a once-in-a-lifetime chance at him. We can't make a mistake."

"You're right, but man, it's tough," John said.

Sam replied, "I know, but think about it. It's the first day. The elk are in almost the exact same area as we saw them a week ago. Nobody else is in the area. So unless we blow it and push them out, they're staying close."

John nodded. "Yeah, that makes sense, but I have to tell you, I was trembling when just the raghorn and spike walked by us. I can't imagine that big bull that close. I think I'd shit my pants."

Sam laughed. "No doubt, it's going to happen, and it will probably happen fast. You're going to be fine, buddy."

Sam and John enjoyed their lunch and relaxed. Occasionally, they'd hike back up the trail and check the wind. Each time the wind was swirling in every direction, and they would return down the trail to their packs.

After a while, Sam said, "I don't know. It seems like it's getting worse, not better. We might have to try again tomorrow. Let's give it a little time, another hour or so."

The next time they hiked up, Sam decided to hike up further where they could see the elk. They were still there, and the big bull was lying in a small open spot.

Sam said excitedly, "Jesus, he's a great bull, but he's in a bad spot. We'd better wait." Just then, Sam noticed the wind was picking up.

"That's it. John, let's head back down to the cabin. We'll get him in the morning."

"Okay, buddy, whatever you think."

Sam and John loaded their packs and headed back toward the cabin. Sam strapped his bow on the back of his pack, but John decided he'd carry his.

CHAPTER 21

With plenty of daylight left, Sam and John took their time going down the trail. Quietly and carefully, Sam and John watched each step.

John stopped not far from the cabin and quickly got Sam's attention. When Sam turned around, John was hunched down and knocking an arrow in his bow. Then he pointed down the drop-off on the downhill side of the trail. Below them was a mixture of berry bushes and tall fir trees.

John looked at Sam and again pointed down below him, but this time, he mouthed, "Big buck."

Sam got down and didn't dare move so he wouldn't spook the buck. Of course, he couldn't see it from where he was, but he watched as John attached his bow release to the loop on his string and drew back his bow.

Sam thought John was shitting him, something they both got a kick out of doing to each other.

Then John slowly rose up and released the arrow. The Mathews bow rotated forward in John's left hand, and Sam heard a loud smack and then something crashing in the brush.

Sam still didn't move and watched John excitedly pumping his fist, saying, "Yes, yes!" John motioned Sam to him and said, "He's down right in front of me. He's big, Sam." Sam walked to the edge of the trail and looked down into the brush and berry bushes. A huge mule deer buck was piled up on the ground just twenty-five yards away. Sam couldn't believe it. "Holy shit, John, he's a monster!"

John had just shot the biggest buck in his life, and it almost dropped in its tracks. Both men dropped their packs and scrambled down the steep bank to the buck.

The big mountain muley had four tall, heavy points on each side. His main beams were thick, dark, and wide.

Sam shook John's hand. "Congratulations, buddy, nice job. That's one hell of a buck."

John could hardly talk. He was so excited. "He was looking right at me and standing broadside. I about shit myself when I saw him."

Sam climbed back up to his pack and removed the camera and tripod from John's pack. He snapped a few pictures of John and the buck before going back down.

"You know, John, you have to have a shoulder mount done on this guy."

John held up the buck's head and could believe it. Then he said, "Hell yeah, he's going on the wall."

"Alright, Buddy, let's get some pictures." Sam snapped pictures as John posed with his trophy, then set up the tripod and set the timer. Then he hurried down next to John and shook his hand.

"John, we're probably only a thousand yards from the trailhead. That big blow-down is right around the corner."

"I know. I still can't believe it."

John and Sam reached down and grabbed the buck's antlers. Then together, they dragged the buck out of the heavy brush to have more room to field dress the buck.

Sam asked John to go back up to their packs and get the pack frames, and his game saw out of his backpack.

"Grab the game bags, too, and I'll get started," Sam said.

Sam was an expert at field dressing and caping out big game, with years of experience hunting big game and taxidermy. Sam quickly pulled the hide and cape back off the shoulders and neck. Leaving plenty of room for a shoulder mount. John separated the head from the body with Sam's saw and moved it to the side.

John had never field-dressed a deer to pack out on a pack frame. Usually, John would gut out a deer, dragging it out to the truck or loading the whole animal onto a game cart.

John watched as Sam worked with precision along the back, exposing the thick back straps.

Sam said, "Alright, buddy, take your time and cut off the back straps and put them in a game bag." John took his new skinning knife and followed Sam's instructions. Like a pro, John had the thick cuts of meat off the backbone and in a game bag.

The steep downhill shot that dropped the big buck in its tracks had entered high on the buck's back and sliced into its spinal cord, then exited out the buck's rib cage. It was a lethal shot but just two inches higher, and it would have missed.

Sam went to work on the hind quarters and shoulders, and the two men had the buck stripped of all its meat in no time.

"Let's drag the carcass farther down into the trees," Sam suggested. "Dinner bells are going to be ringing, and if there is a bear in the area, he's going to find it."

John and Sam dragged the carcass down the steep slope until they came to a small rocky ledge. "Awesome, Let's toss it down there, John."

When the carcass had tumbled over the ledge, John asked, "You think that's good enough, Sam?"

"Yeah, we just need to be careful when we come by here."

When they returned to their packs and climbed back to the trail with the first load of meat, John made two more trips to retrieve the other game bags and the buck's head and cape. Once on the trail, they helped each other lift the pack frames onto their backs. Sam was packing one of the hindquarters, and John had the game bag full of backstraps and the huge buck's head and cape.

Leaving their backpacks on the trail with the two other game bags, they picked up their bows and started back toward the cabin. Except for crawling over the downed trees along the way, they quickly made it to the trailhead and the cabin.

When they finally got to Sam's truck. John said, "Wow, that didn't take us long."

"No, it didn't. We were even closer than I'd thought," Sam replied as he lowered his pack onto the tailgate.

"Hey buddy, didn't the guy at the store say he was going to say open a little longer during hunting season?"

John said, "Yeah, he did, but he also pointed out where he lived and said if the store was closed, we could come to his house and get him. Then he'd open up the freezer for us."

Sam said. "Awesome! We need to do that. With how hot it is, we need to keep the meat cool. Plus, it won't take long in this heat for the hair on the cape to slip and ruin it."

"Sounds like a plan, buddy."

In the truck bed, Sam had a big cooler with five blocks of ice, and they put the bag of back straps and a hind quarter inside. Then they returned to the trail and started the short hike to retrieve the rest of their gear and meat.

Just carrying their empty pack frames, the hike was easy, and soon they were tying the remaining game bags on the frames. Then both men picked up their backpacks and left for the cabin.

Once back at the truck, they loaded the game bags into the truck bed and put their bows and backpacks in the back seat. Next, Sam went into the cabin and grabbed a couple of drinks. Then he and John sat in the camp chairs and relaxed before they made the trip down to Blake.

Sam reached over to John and shook his hand. "Not too bad of an opening day hunt."

With a huge smile, John said, "Amazing, I still can't believe we found your bull, and I shot my biggest buck ever. Not a bad day at all, buddy."

After just a few minutes, Sam and John got in the truck and headed down the road.

They were lucky, and when they got to Blake, the owner was just closing, and they were able to catch him before he left.

"Hey John, hey Sam. Back so soon, Did you get something?" Randy asked.

John smiled and said, "Yeah, we got a hell of a buck and were hoping we could use your freezer."

"No problem, just pull your truck around back, and I'll open the door." John walked around the store to the back, and Sam drove around to the back door.

When Randy walked out the back door, he spotted the huge rack sticking up above the side of the bed. "Looks like you did get a nice one. Who shot it?"

John smiled and quickly said, "I did."

Randy helped Sam and John get the game bags and head into the walk-in freezer. Sam said, "I sure appreciate you doing this for us."

Randy replied, "You're welcome. I've got plenty of room." Sam shook Randy's hand.

Then he said, "Well, you're saving us a long trip back home."

"Can I give you some money for your trouble?" John asked.

"Oh, hell no, it's no trouble. I'm just glad to help you out." Randy quickly replied.

Sam said, "Thanks again, Randy. It's made things a lot easier for us. But I guess we'd better take off. I've got a date with a big bull."

"You're welcome, guys. Drive safe and good luck."

CHAPTER 22

L ate Sunday morning, Jake and Wyatt arrived at Dan's office. They both said, "Morning, Dan."

"Morning, guys," Dan replied. "Did you get a chance to sleep in?"

Wyatt chuckled and said, "Yeah, thanks for that. I needed my beauty sleep."

Jokingly Jake said, "You should have slept longer."

Dan and Jake both laughed at the witty comment. Wyatt laughed and plopped down in a chair.

Dan had his laptop packed up on the desk, lying on a black rifle case. Inside was an F.N. patrol carbine.

Dan said, "I'm ready to go, guys. There's a small armory downstairs if you need anything."

Wyatt said, "Nope, we've got everything we need."

"I figured you did. Are you good, Jake?"

"Yeah, I'm good, boss."

"Alright then, guys, let's get your gear loaded up in the Yukon, and we'll get going."

"Are we heading straight to the lodge?" Jake asked.

"Yeah, we'll get settled in and see if we can meet up with Sheriff Taylor. He said to call him, and he'd meet us there."

Jake replied, "Sounds good, Dan."

Dan was driving a Black GMC Yukon. Jake pulled over next to it and popped open the trunk. The first thing Wyatt grabbed was a black F.N. rifle case. Dan said, "I see you brought the Scar."

"Yes sir, you know me. I don't leave home without it. What with the firepower these assholes are packing, we might need it to even the score."

"Let's hope not, but I'm glad you have it," Dan replied.

After Jake and Wyatt finished loading their gear, the three agents left for Libby. The quickest way was north up highway ninety-three, which would take them past Flathead Lake into Kalispell, then to Libby, but Dan decided they would take the state highway to Thompson Falls, then cut across the highway north to Blake and into Libby. Taking that route would allow them to see what they had flown over the day before. Libby was a hundred and fifty miles away, twenty miles north of Blake, and would take two, maybe three hours to get there. Along the way, they would travel along the Clark Fork River.

The Clark Fork begins its journey from the mountains near Butte, Montana, winding its way northwest before entering Pend Oreile Lake in northern Idaho.

~ ~ ~

It was quiet in the Yukon as the three agents took in the sights along the river and the massive rock formations of the rugged mountain valley. After passing through several small towns, Wyatt spotted a road sign saying, '*Thompson Falls twenty miles.*'

"Let's stop and get lunch, Dan."

"Sounds great. I was thinking the same thing." Dan replied.

A short series of tight, windy corners were coming up, and the road narrowed with the river on one side and a rock wall on the other. Dan noticed a game crossing sign a mile back that said 'Big Horn Sheep.' Suddenly, from around the second corner, three Big Horn Rams stood right on the road's edge. Dan slowed to a crawl, and the three agents stared out their windows at the sheep as they passed.

Jake said, "Well, you don't see that in Seattle."

Excited, Wyatt said, "That's crazy; I don't think I've ever seen bighorn sheep that close."

Dan sighed. "That sure in hell would ruin your day hitting one of them."

"Boy, I guess," Jake said.

When they finally got to Thompson Falls, they stopped at a small diner for lunch, then continued their drive another ten miles toward the turn-off to Blake.

When they reached the highway and turned north, the scenery quickly changed to thick pines lining the highway. In places, a small river wound its way alongside the road. Groves of cedar trees on the edge of the road almost made it look like you were in a tunnel of trees. When the route entered large meadows, the men could see the tall, majestic peaks of the Cabinet mountains. The sky was bright blue, and the snow-capped peaks glistened in the sun.

"My God, this is amazing," Jake proclaimed.

Wyatt said, "Yeah, it's pretty damn awesome. You can drop me off anywhere, Dan. Just leave me a fishing pole."

"I wish I could, buddy." Dan said, "Maybe someday all three of us can come back and drag T.J. over here with us."

Wyatt said, "That would be awesome. I bet T.J. would love it."

Twenty miles from Blake, they passed a small sign that said '*Trapper Creek*.' Then just a few miles from Blake, they passed a paved driveway going off into thick timber. They didn't know how close they had just come to Bishop, Barnes, and Becker.

After they drove through the small town of Blake, it was only a short time before they pulled into the parking lot at the Snowshoe Peak Lodge. Dan was surprised. "Man, T.J. went all-out this time."

Jake replied, "Boy, I guess. This place is pretty damn fancy."

Excitedly, Wyatt said, "I bet they have an awesome pool."

Dan laughed, "I don't think we'll have time for the pool."

Jokingly, Wyatt said, "I forgot my swimsuit anyways."

All three men laughed. Then once Dan parked, he got out his phone. "Hey, why don't you guys go in and get our rooms? I'm going to give Sheriff Taylor a call."

"You got it, boss," Jake replied.

The sheriff picked up on the second ring. "Sheriff Taylor, this is Agent Dan Black."

"Agent Black, I've been waiting for your call." Sheriff Taylor replied.

"We made it to the lodge, and my team is checking us into the rooms.

"What lodge is that at, agent?'

"You can call me Dan. And it's the Snowshoe Peak Lodge just west of Libby. Do you know the place?"

"Yes, sir, pretty fancy place. It looks like the Bureau is taking pretty good care of you."

Dan laughed. "Where are you?"

"I'm in Libby; getting there will only take a few minutes."

"Sounds good. See you then."

Wyatt and Jake came back out to the Yukon.

Jake said, "We're good to go, boss. Did you get in touch with the sheriff?"

"I did. He'll be here in a few minutes. I'll wait for him. Is there a private conference room or somewhere we can sit down and talk?"

Jake said, "Yeah, there is. It looks like T.J. thought of everything. Your room has an office."

"Alright, can you guys haul our gear in and meet me in my room?" Jake replied, "Sure thing."

CHAPTER 23

On the way to the lodge, Officer Taylor wondered about his captain's arrangements with the FBI agents. His captain didn't think much about the FBI being around, blowing off the idea that the fugitives were still in the area. Jim wasn't sure either, and he felt like he would be a babysitter or tour guide. Still, Jim had been in contact with two game wardens in the area and informed them what he would be doing in the Blake area. He also knew that two highway patrol officers nearby could respond to his call if needed.

When he arrived at the lodge, he quickly spotted the black Yukon. Dan was standing next to it, leaning against the hood.

The officer exited his truck, and Dan greeted him with a firm handshake. "Officer Taylor?"

"Yes, sir. You must be Agent Black."

"I am, but please just call me Dan. I really don't care to hear the 'agent' stuff constantly."

"Good enough, Dan. In that case, I'm Jim."

"Well, Jim, let's go inside, and I'll introduce you to the other guys."

In the lodge, Dan noticed Wyatt in the gift shop. "Wyatt, what are you doing?"

Jokingly, Wyatt said, "Well, looking for a souvenir, of course."

Dan just shook his head and looked at Jim. "Well, that's Wyatt. He's a big kid at heart, but trust me, there's no better man to have to watch your back when things go wrong."

Wyatt walked over to Jim and shook his hand. "I'm Wyatt; welcome to the team."

"Thanks, I'm Jim. I guess I am on loan to you guys."

Wyatt looked at Dan and said, "Honestly, I was just hanging out waiting for you so I could give you the key to your room."

"Really, then what's in the bag?"

Wyatt laughed. "It's a swimsuit."

In Dan's room, Jake was waiting in the small office. "Jake, this is Sheriff Jim Taylor."

"Pleasure to meet you, sheriff."

"Same here, Jake."

"Alright, guys, now that we have all the introductions over, grab a chair." Dan said, "Jim, do you have any questions for my guys or me?"

"No, not really. My captain already briefed me, and I understand we are going to knock on some doors in the Blake area.

"That's it. Do you know much about the area?"

"A little, it's not my normal patrol area. There are a lot of vacant summer homes. If you don't mind, what makes you think the fugitives are still in the area?"

"Just a hunch. It's been digging at me for a few days."

"Well, that's good enough for me. So I have no problem with that."

Wyatt slapped his knee. "Hey, I like this guy already."

"Jim, where are you staying," Dan asked.

"I've got a room at the Super 8 in Libby."

Dan immediately said, "Jake, if you would go down to the front office with Jim, get him a room here."

"Hell yeah," Wyatt proclaimed

Jim said, "That's not necessary; I'm fine."

"It's no big deal, Jim. It's on the Bureau."

"Alright, Dan, Sounds good. Thank you."

"After you check in, come back to the room," Dan said. "I want to review a few maps and get everyone on the same page about tomorrow."

After they left, Wyatt asked, "Well, boss, what do you think?"

"He seems like a decent enough guy. I appreciate him teaming up with us."

"Yeah, at least he doesn't seem like some asshole."

On the way to the front office, Jim asked, "If it's alright, what can you tell me about Dan?"

"No problem, that's fair enough. Dan's not some stuffed shirt agent. Don't get me wrong; he's all business and one of the best field agents in the country. He knows what he's doing, and you can trust every word he says. I admire the guy. As you can probably tell, we aren't your typical FBI agents."

Jim replied, "I can tell you guys are a tight group."

"Me and Wyatt, we've been together since serving in Afghanistan. Wyatt's like a brother to me."

After Jake and Jim returned to the room, Dan laid out National Forest and landowner maps on the desk. He and Wyatt were drawing up a grid search north of Blake.

"Jim, did you get all checked in?" Dan asked.

"Sure did, Dan. Thanks again."

"No problem, Jim. Looking at these maps, what can you tell us about the area? We flew over the area yesterday, and it looks like roads are everywhere."

Jim replied, "As I said, I'm not real familiar with the area, but a lot of the roads are forest roads and a few gated logging roads," Pointing at the map, Jim said, "The area north of Blake has quite a few off-the-grid vacation homes. There's no power, but most have solar panels and propane. The forest service bought up a few older abandoned places years ago."

Dan asked, "Does anybody live there year-round?"

"There are a few residents who live closer to town year-round," Jim replied. "Twenty-five miles south of Blake, you start running into small ranches that operate year-round, some of which provide guide services into the wilderness."

"What about closer to Blake? We saw a lot of paved driveways on our way here."

"Yeah, that's where you find the million-dollar getaways. Especially closer to the lake. You know, it will take a few days to check them all."

"I plan on it. What else can you tell us?"

"That's about it, Dan."

"Thanks, Jim," said Dan. "Alright, guys, I'm going to call T.J. and check-in. Then I'm going to head down to the restaurant for dinner. It looks like a hell of a place to eat. I'll meet up with you guys there. My treat."

Jake and Wyatt both said, "Sounds good, boss."

While Dan, Jake, and Jim sat at a table in the restaurant, waiting for Wyatt, Dan and Jake looked around at all the shoulder mounts displayed on the huge log walls. A giant bull elk hung on the wall above their table. A life-sized mount of a massive grizzly stood on all fours at the entrance. When the waitress handed the men their menus, Wyatt came strolling in wearing a t-shirt, his new swimsuit, and his unlaced boots.

Dan shook his head and couldn't help but laugh. Jake and Jim stared at him, and they laughed as Wyatt took a seat at the table.

"Did you guys order yet?"

Dan handed Wyatt a menu. "Well, you look comfortable, Wyatt."

Wyatt took the menu and said, "I am, thanks. I'm starved."

Jake said jokingly, "Well, buddy, that's quite the outfit, Wyatt, with your boots and all."

"Thanks, they didn't have any flip-flops in the gift shop."

"I guess you're going for a swim after dinner," Dan said.

"Hell yeah, you guys should join me. The gift shop is still open."

Dan replied, "No thanks, buddy, I'm good."

After dinner, Wyatt got up to leave for the pool. "What time are we heading out in the morning, Dan?"

"Early, I'd like to be knocking on doors by seven. So let's meet up at the Yukon by six."

"Sounds great. I'll see you guys then." Wyatt said.

Dan asked Jim if there was someplace close by where they could get something to take with them for lunch tomorrow. Jim replied yes; back in Libby, there was a twenty-four-hour grocery store with a small deli where they could get ready-made sandwiches and snacks. Then Dan asked Jake and Jim if they would go and get what they needed. Both men agreed and told Dan they would see him in the morning.

~ ~ ~

Jake, Wyatt, and Jim waited outside by the black Yukon the following morning. There were only three other vehicles in the parking lot. It was the off-season and a slow time at the lodge. It wouldn't be busy until the heavy snow blanketed the nearby ski resort and the lodge filled with anxious skiers and snowboarders.

Dan wasn't surprised when he saw the three men outside. He knew Jake and even Wyatt were going to be all business today. It was a warm morning, and the sky was clear, with only a few clouds lingering over the mountains. Dressed in jeans and his on-duty shirt, Sheriff Jim Taylor could sense the serious change in mood of the agents. Also dressed in jeans and blue T-shirts with large yellow letters' FBI' on the front and back, Jake and Wyatt greeted Dan as he approached the Yukon. "Good morning, boss."

"Good morning, guys, How are you, Jim?"

"I'm good, Dan."

"Well, guys, let's get going. I'm going to ride with Jim. Jake, Wyatt, you take the Yukon." Then, looking at Jim, Dan said, "Jim, I'm not sure how it will play out if we come up on these guys. But they will be heavily armed with automatic weapons, and I don't expect them to surrender. It will get serious fast. It's important that you stay with me and listen to everything I say. Then, in a situation where we have to make an entry, Wyatt and Jake will take point."

Jim replied, "I understand, Dan."

"Alright, guys, Jake, Wyatt, you follow us."

Only a short time later, the four men turned south toward Blake. Then, finally, they came across the first road leading to a home and a small garage hidden in tall pines. It looked peaceful and quiet.

No vehicles were in sight, and Dan instructed Jim to pull up fifty yards from the home. Jake pulled up next to Jim, and all four men got out.

Dan walked up to the door and knocked. "FBI." It was quiet. Again, Dan knocked and repeated, "FBI." Dan motioned Jake and Jim to the garage and Wyatt to the back of the home. After, they searched the area and peered into every window. Dan was satisfied, and the men moved on. Over and over again, the same scene played out as Dan directed his search.

Several times they were met with a locked gate, and the four men would leave their vehicles and proceed on foot to conduct the search. It was taking time, but Dan covered every road and every home. There was no joking around—no talking about the beautiful homes and scenery. Jim was amazed at how focused all three agents were on the task.

It wasn't until they pulled off onto a gated logging road for lunch that the mood changed. Dan said. "I don't know, guys. This could be a big waste of time."

Jake said, "Boss, I don't think so. I have a feeling we are on the right track."

Wyatt added, "Me too; let's stick to it. We'll catch a break."

Dan took the maps and put them on the tailgate of the truck. Then with a red marker, he crossed off every road and home they had already searched.

"I just wish we had more guys."

Jake said, "You know, Boss, if you're not feeling right, we can always pull in another team. They could probably be here by tomorrow afternoon."

"I know, but really, guys, I may just be wrong. I was hoping for more local support. No offense, Jim."

"None was taken, I understand, But our departments are pretty small, and the counties are big. So we are running short-handed as it is. I'm surprised they cut me loose."

Dan said, "I hear you, and I appreciate you teaming up with us."

"I do have a little good news, though," Jim said, "Patrolling the Libby area, there are two Highway patrol officers, and south of Blake, there are two Montana fish and game wardens on patrol. I talked to them briefly and filled them in on what we were doing. They assured me they would be able to respond if needed."

"That sounds good, Jim. Thank you."

After lunch, the four men continued their search of the area, but again they came up empty-handed.

Getting late, Dan called it off, and they all returned to the lodge.

~   ~   ~

Once again, Wyatt, Jake, and Jim meet with Dan in the small office in his room. Dan laid out the map and pointed out the circles on the map.

Dan placed his finger over one of the circles just one mile from Blake. "The way I figure it, guys, by late afternoon tomorrow, we'll be here." Circled under his finger was the abandoned house where Bishop, Barnes, and Becker had first taken refuge.

CHAPTER 24

Monday morning, Sam built another fire outside of the cabin. He was surprised that John was already up and getting ready to go. Sam sat by the fire, hoping the big bull was still in the area.

When John walked over to the fire and sat down, Sam poured him a cup of coffee. "Good morning, buddy. How did you sleep?"

"Morning Sam, I slept like a rock. How about you?"

"I tossed and turned, thinking about the bull."

"Well, I think today is the day, Sam."

Then John noticed Sam's day pack and pack frame on the truck's tailgate with his bow already strapped on the back.

"You aren't taking your big pack?" John asked.

"No, just the day pack and pack frame, we need to make better time getting up there this morning. I'd like to be up there before they bed down."

"Sounds like a plan," John agreed, "Do you want to have freeze-dried food for breakfast?"

"Yeah, let's do that. I'll get some water boiling."

"Alright, I'll get things swapped over to my day-pack."

After a quick breakfast and extinguishing the fire, Sam and John again left for the trailhead. After climbing over the downed trees, it wasn't long before they approached where John had shot his huge buck. Both men released the snaps on their chest holsters, then, with their headlamps, looked above and below them as they passed by, making sure they wouldn't be surprised by a charging bear.

Sam picked up the pace and was making good time, stopping here and there to catch his breath and grab a drink of water. They heard crashing in the dark timber several times along the way, thinking it was just deer they had spooked. They would take a glance and continue their hike.

It was warm, and they had to wipe the sweat from their foreheads each time they stopped. Finally, at the trail to the lake, Sam and John took a longer break and sat down alongside the trail. It was already getting light, but they were getting close. Both men opened energy bars and snacked on some beef jerky. Sam and John unstrapped their bows, then continued up the last couple of switchbacks. Sam's pace slowed, and then he paused to check the wind. It was dead still; not even a slight breeze blew through the treetops. Sam turned and gave John a thumbs-up.

When they reached the ridge line overlooking the small valley and open meadows where the ground began to level off, Sam rechecked the wind. Nothing, no wind. "Let's leave out pack frames here and just take our packs."

"Sounds good to me."

Sam slowly crept over to where he could see down into the meadows and the creek bottom, hoping to spot the herd of elk they'd spotted yesterday.

John silently eased beside Sam, now sitting down, glassing the valley and distant ridge tops. Then quietly, he whispered, "Anything?"

Sam shook his head no and continued to glass. Then, suddenly, Sam's head snapped to his left.

Glassing hard into the timber, he saw two mule deer easing their way toward the small creek.

Ten minutes passed, then Sam motioned to John for them to move farther down the ridge. Again they took their time and watched each step. Finally, when they'd reached where they had spotted the bull yesterday, they sat down, and both men glassed the ridges.

Suddenly, a deep raspy bugle followed by three quick, heavy grunts echoed through the timber. It was the same tone and raspy bugle they watched come from the big bull the day before. Sam knew it had to be the big seven-point bull, and he was close. But this time, the bugle came from the tall ridge just ahead of them above the trail to the right.

Sam quickly but quietly positioned himself to see up the ridge. John didn't move and slipped his cow call into his mouth.

Sam turned around and had John ease his way toward him, whispering for him to be silent. It was quiet, and Sam rechecked the wind. It was perfect. Sam couldn't see around two giant yellow pines in front of him, blocking his view of the ridge. Sam whispered for John to follow him.

When they reached the big trees and had a clear view of the ridge, cow elk dotted the timber and huge open areas high above the trail. A deep game trail wound down from the ridge, three hundred yards ahead of Sam and John, before slipping over the hiking trail and down to the creek bottom.

Suddenly, the huge seven-point bull stepped out into the clear and released another low, slow bugle. He was almost nine hundred yards up the ridge, surrounded by his herd of cows. Sticks and twigs were tangled in his heavy rack.

Sam knew there was no way the big bull would come to any call. He and John would have to find the right spot to set up an ambush. It would be a waiting game, and Sam needed to quickly figure out where to set up once the elk began to move.

An hour passed and then another. Still, the elk refused to give up their intentions. Finally, Sam noticed a small game trail just below him that slanted down into the thick timber and knew it had to meet up with the game trail that came down the ridge.

After pointing the trail out to John, Sam turned his attention back to the bull and herd of cows. He hoped that with the sun beating down on the elk, it wouldn't be much longer until they moved and started following the trail down into thick, cool timber and willows that lined Trapper Creek just three hundred yards below him.

Suddenly, John spotted the same raghorn bull emerging from the timber above the big bull. Then, following closely behind, five more cows made their appearance.

They passed by the big bull and slowly started down the game trail. Then several more cows and calves eased their way toward the trail.

Quickly, Sam turned to John and again pointed at the small game trail. Then, whispering, he said to John, "Let's move and cut them off."

Sam and John slowly slipped over the edge and onto the small trail a moment later. Out of sight of the elk, they hurried into the timber, slowly easing over the downed trees. Sam was right, and as they peaked over a slight rise, the heavily-used game trail was only fifty yards away. Sam eased his way silently to a large, downed tree five, maybe ten yards above and twenty-five yards away from the trail, giving him a perfect view and shot path. John took cover behind two large pines twenty yards above Sam and perhaps thirty feet farther down, toward the creek.

He watched as Sam knelt on his right knee and dug the heel of his left boot into the ground. John's excitement rose when he watched Sam notch his arrow.

Sam felt his heart racing when elk started appearing on the trail and in the timber in front of him. Suddenly the low, raspy bugle ripped through the trees. The massive bull was on the move. Then another low bugle followed by heavy grunts gave away the position of the big bull. He was a hundred yards away and on a slow, steady walk down the trail.

Sam strained his eyes and caught a glimpse of the enormous bull. Sam's heart raced. He took a slow deep breath, then attached his release to the loop on his string. Sam could see the huge rack scraping against the trees as the bull got closer and closer. The bull wouldn't clear for a shot until he was thirty yards away or closer. After that, it would be an easy shot.

Sam had practiced all summer with his bow; at that range, he could send three arrows into an area no bigger than a dime.

Sam carefully scanned the bull with his range finder. Eighty yards—just fifty more, and Sam would take down a giant, record-class bull with a bow.

Sam fought to get his breathing under control. Twenty, maybe thirty elk filed through the trees in front of him. Then, out of nowhere, the big six-point bull Sam and John had spotted the day before crashed through the timber and stopped only twenty yards from Sam. The bull was looking directly at John. John kept utterly motionless, afraid even to blink. There was no way the bull could see him. Suddenly a squirrel scampered across a log a few feet from John, flicking his tail and barking in protest at John's presence.

Only moving his eyes, Sam looked back toward the seven-point. He was only ten yards from the small clearing and Sam's shot window. He was standing motionless, staring at the bull just ahead of him. Sam knew the hunt could end any second, and both bulls would disappear.

Suddenly, the six-point turned his head back to the trail and slowly walked into the cool, thick timber. Sam's bull stood still, not moving. Then he shook his huge rack back and forth before walking slowly down the trail at thirty-five yards when the bull walked behind a massive pine. Sam went to full draw and waited. The bull's pace was picking up, and at thirty yards, John gave out a single short call of a lost calf. The huge bull stopped broadside and looked in the direction of the call.

Sam softly squeezed the release. The razor-sharp broadhead hit its mark, slicing into hide and muscle, then ripped through the bull's lungs before coming to rest in the ground on the other side of his thick chest.

The bull lunged forward and charged down the trail into the timber and out of Sam's sight. John saw the bull fifty yards away stumble and come to a stop. Gasping for air, he slowly rocked back and forth. Then the giant bull collapsed.

"He's down, Sam! He's down!" John exclaimed with excitement while pumping his fist. Then he looked at Sam, who was shaking his bow above his head.

"Oh my god, buddy, you got him."

Sam dropped to the ground, overcome with excitement, and clutched his head in his hands. John hurried over, knelt on one knee, and placed his hand on Sam's shoulder. "Holy crap, Sam, you got him."

Sam took a deep breath. "I can't believe it, John. We got him."

"You got him, Sam. He's down!"

Then John helped Sam to his feet, and they both walked down to the trail to where Sam had made the shot.

John picked up the blood-soaked arrow and handed it to Sam. John said, "It was a perfect shot."

Excited, Sam replied, "You stopped him right in front of me. I still can't believe it."

John knew exactly where the bull had fallen and pointed it out to Sam. "He's piled up just over there, just fifty yards away, almost on the trail."

John followed Sam as they walked towards the bull. Excited, John said, "Holy shit, he's as big as a horse. My god, he's huge."

Sam reached out and shook John's hand. "Thank you for being here, John."

"You bet, buddy."

"I told you you'd be shocked when you saw a bull on the ground."

"I know, My god, he's massive."

With a huge smile, Sam said, "Well, now the work starts, but first, it's picture time."

Sam removed his pack and withdrew his camera while John set up the tripod. Sam laid his bow across the bull's chest and struggled to lift his head and massive rack.

John walked over and helped, then rolled a small log up against the bull's neck.

"Alright, buddy, say cheese." Then John took picture after picture of Sam and the bull. Sam never quit smiling as he examined the rack. "He has to be at least fifty inches wide, and both sides are a perfect match."

The big seven-point 'imperial' bull was the trophy of a lifetime. Its long tines, and heavy mass carried far up his main beams.

"He's going to score in the three-nineties, maybe even four hundred class, John."

Sam walked over and took the camera from John. "Okay, buddy, get over there." John posed with both hands holding the massive rack, and Sam snapped pictures of his best friend.

Then Sam set up the camera on the tripod and called John over, showing him how to set the timer. Then he went over and positioned himself behind the bull. "Okay, after you hit the timer, you'll have fifteen seconds to get over here."

John pushed the button and hurriedly took his position kneeling beside Sam.

"Sweet," Sam said. "Let's do a couple more. Then we have to get to work."

After the pictures, Sam said, "Well, I hate to tell you, but you need to climb back up and get the pack frames."

Smiling, John replied, "No problem."

"I'll get started caping him out."

"Sounds good. I'll be right back." Then John took off toward the small game trail and started up the three-hundred-yard climb to the top of the ridge.

When he returned, Sam had the cape pulled up high on the bull's neck and was carefully caping out the head.

There was no reason to carry the whole head out. The cape and antlers alone would be heavy enough.

"How's it going?" John asked.

"I'm just about done. Next, we'll start boning out all the meat. Stretch the trap out, and we'll toss the meat on it."

Then Sam got the bone saw out of his pack, and John helped hold the antlers while Sam sawed through the skull and separated the skull cap and antlers from the head.

Then, Sam took his knife, scooped out the upper portion of the bull's brain into his hand, and held it out to John. "Here you go, buddy."

"What?"

"You have to take a bite."

"Oh, hell no!"

Sam looked serious. "Come on. It's a tradition."

"No way, really?"

Sam tossed the chunk of brain into the bushes and busted out laughing.

"Asshole, I almost did it."

Sam laughed uncontrollably and just shook his head.

Then John rolled the bull to where Sam could finish removing its skin. Together they carved away at the strips of back strap and tossed them onto the tarp.

Then Sam separated the hind and front quarters and carefully removed the flank steaks. "Almost done, buddy. We just have to bone out the hind quarters, and then we can pack it all up."

The average weight of elk hind quarters with bone-in is easily sixty-five pounds, but this was no average bull, and the weight had to be closer to seventy-five—way too much to pack out on your back. So even boned out, it was going to be rough.

After they had all the meat in the game bags and the first load tied to their pack frames, John asked, "What's your plan?"

"I don't know. I think we should bite the bullet, pack everything up to the ridge, and get it over with."

"Sounds good, buddy."

Sam helped John with his pack. Then John lifted Sam's pack onto his friend's shoulder. Carrying their bows, they made the first trip to the top of the ridge and found a place to unload the packs in the shade. After three more trips, they finally had everything on top. Sam and John were exhausted and lay flat on their backs, staring at the clear blue sky. A light breeze blew across the treetops, and both men focused on a small white cloud drifting across the sky directly above them.

John took a deep breath. "I still can't believe it. I thought the six-point bull had me busted."

"Me too, it was pretty intense. We got lucky."

"Yeah, it was crazy. I thought for sure he saw me."

Both men relaxed in the shade of the huge pine a few feet from the trail.

John said, "Man, I could sure use a nap."

Sam laughed and said, "I wish, but we need to get going. We've got to get this meat on some ice."

Sam slowly got to his feet and stretched out his back while taking a long deep breath through his nose. Sam looked around for a decent tree to hang the game bags on, but there wasn't anything nearby with limbs low enough to get a rope over. Unfortunately, the only tree with low enough limbs and offered shade was up the trail and twenty yards back down the ridge. Sam pointed it out to John and said, "Well, it sucks, but it looks like the best place for shade."

"I guess we'd better grab some rope and get things off the ground," John replied.

After getting several ropes out of his day pack, John helped move the game bags under the tree, then tied a rock to the end of each rope. It took a few tries, but finally, three ropes hung over the branches. Then they hoisted two heavy game bags full of meat ten feet off the ground.

"You think that's high enough?" John asked.

"I hope so, but I don't think we have to worry about it. If a bear shows up, he'll probably get on the carcass."

Then John and Sam hoisted up the massive rack, and the bull's cape rolled up in another game bag.

Sam said, "Well, here we go. It's going to take three trips, and we'd better make them quick. I'm really worried about the meat spoiling in this heat." Then they each slipped a couple of water bottles into the cargo pockets of their hunting pants,

"Well, at least it's all downhill from here," John replied as he lifted his loaded-down pack frame, then helped Sam do the same.

"Holy crap, you ready for this, John?"

Smiling, John said, "Not really, but I guess I don't have a choice."

Both men had their bows tied to the backs of their heavy packs and headed down the first switchback. Sam's trekking poles helped a lot, but he still felt the strain on his back, especially his knee. But Sam never complained as they quickly rounded each corner to the next switchback, pausing several times and resting their packs on logs, rocks, anything they could find to take the weight off their shoulders, not wanting to take off the packs.

They were surprised at how quickly they got to where John had taken down the buck the day before.

John stopped for a second, looked over the trial's edge, then said, "Wow, we're making great time."

"Yeah, not bad. We might even be able to get everything packed out before dark."

After climbing over the downed trees across the trail again, they finally saw the trail marker. Excited, John said, "Holy crap, we cruised down the trail."

"Man, I guess it didn't seem that bad."

When they got to the truck and lowered the packs onto the tailgate, they put the game bags into the biggest cooler and covered them with ice.

Sam said, "Alright, just two more trips and we're done."

"Are we going to take it home?" John asked.

"Hell no, I bet that six-point bull didn't go far. We'll find him."

"You think so?"

"There's a good chance. I want to set you up for a shot on that bull."

"That would be unreal," John exclaimed, "Two big bulls and a monster muley. Holy crap!"

"We'll just take the meat and cape to Blake and get an early start in the morning. The hunt isn't over, buddy."

"Cool beans, sounds awesome."

Sam took his bow and put it in the truck's back seat.

"I'm leaving my bow, and I think I'll change into shorts."

"That sounds great, but I'm going to take my bow."

"Oh, hell yeah."

John and Sam went into the cabin and changed, then grabbed a quick bite to eat and a cold drink.

"Are you ready, John?" Sam asked before finishing off his ice-cold Coke.

"Yep, round two."

Once again, Sam took the lead at the trailhead and quickly passed through the difficult section of downed trees and limbs before taking a short break. After the break, Sam started picking up a grueling pace. Looking straight ahead, Sam picked out landmarks on the trail ahead and began counting his steps to himself. "*One, two, three, four, five, six, seven, eight, nine, ten...*" Then would start his cadence all over again. The same thing he did every morning for months during his five a.m. hikes in preparation for the hunt.

Fueled by the thoughts of spoiling meat and anxious to get this part of the hunt over, Sam pulled far ahead of John at times, only pausing just long enough for him to catch up.

John was amazed how Sam, at sixty-six, could keep up such a pace.

Except for Sam's knee, he was in great shape and knew how hard he could push himself. Even though John was much younger, on a trail, Sam stretched his friend's endurance.

After only stopping twice, just long enough to sit down and have a quick drink and an energy bar, they passed by the trail to Lost Lake.

"Holy crap, buddy, are you on a mission?" John asked.

Sam laughed. "Yep, I guess so. I just want to get this over with so we can relax at the cabin."

When they arrived at the tree where they'd hung the rest of the meat and antlers, both men took a seat for a short break. Then, almost as quickly as he'd sat down,

Sam got back up and lowered the rope holding his day-pack and one of the game bags of meat.

"Hell, aren't you going to take a break?"

"Yeah, but I can't help it. I've got to walk over and glass a bit. So kick back, I'll be back in a second."

Sam grabbed his binoculars from his pack and walked over to the edge of the ridgeline. Scanning the far ridges and timber, Sam couldn't believe his eyes. Past the second ridge, high up in an alpine meadow surrounded by aspen and tall fir trees, were more elk. Sam whistled and motioned for John to come over. Sam pointed out the elk, almost a mile away, scattered in the meadow and aspens.

"Do you see the bull?" John asked.

"No, he's not out in the open. I can make out elk in the timber but can't tell what they are. So he's in there somewhere. I guarantee it."

"Holy crap, how are we going to get over there?"

"We will. I don't think they're going anywhere. So we'll get back over here in the morning and make a plan."

"We should take a break tomorrow and come up the next day."

"That's up to you." Then, smiling, Sam said, "I've got my bull."

"You sure did."

"Hey, if we do that, we can drive into Libby to one of the truck stops and grab a quick shower," Sam said. "I must smell like an old, rutting bull elk."

John laughed. "We both do, Sounds like a plan, plus then we can call the wives. I want to check in and see how Lisa is doing."

'Sounds great. Let's get going then." Sam said.

After making the trip down, the trip back up was slower this time, but once they finally arrived at the tree, John lowered another game bag and his day pack. Then after both men had the heavy load tied on the pack frame, they top-loaded their day packs and left back down the trail.

Halfway down, John said, "We're making good time. How's your knee holding up?"

Even though it was killing him, Sam simply replied, "It's fine."

The hike down again was quick. Neither man said a word except for when they took a short break. And even then, Sam would soon resume his hurried cadence.

After returning to the truck, Sam said, "Let's stretch out a tarp and pack the meat up with ice from the other coolers. Then, we can pick up more in Blake." Then, after making sure they tied up the tarp the best they could, Sam said, "Well, one more trip, buddy, but I think we should wait until tomorrow morning."

John took a deep breath and sighed. "I'm good to go if you want."

"I know we made pretty damn good time, I'm surprised, but I think it will be dark by the time we get back up there, packed up, and head back."

"Whatever you think, I'm good either way."

"Yeah, I think we'll wait. Besides, I'm worn out."

"Do you think the cape will be alright?"

"I think it will. It's going to cool off tonight. I can feel it in the knee."

~ ~ ~

Sam was right. That night, a cold front moved in over the mountains, dropping the temperature below freezing in the high country.

The following day when John awoke, he was surprised to see Sam still sleeping and snoring away.

It was cold in the cabin, and John started a fire in the wood stove and then lay back down. An hour passed before Sam rustled out of his sleeping bag.

"Hey John, wake up, buddy."

"I'm awake. I've been listening to you snoring for an hour."

Sam laughed and said, "Good, Consider it payback."

The sun was already up when Sam and John walked out of the cabin. The air was cool and crisp, and a light frost covered the windshield of Sam's truck. Sam started splitting some kindling for a fire, and as John got the coffee pot ready, he said, "Dang, it's kind of chilly this morning."

"Yeah, it really cooled off last night," Sam replied. "Just what we needed."

Taking a big yawn, John asked, "How did you sleep?"

"Man, I slept like a rock," Sam said. "It felt great to sleep in."

"I slept pretty hard too."

Sam smiled at John. "You always do."

"What do you think, Sam? Should we get going?"

"No, as cold as it is, I don't think we have to be in a big rush this morning. We'll have a big breakfast, then head out when we're ready."

After a couple of cups of coffee, Sam cooked a huge breakfast of eggs, bacon, and grits. The two men sat close to the fire, quickly scarfing down their breakfast.

"Well, I suppose we'd better get going. How was your breakfast?" Sam asked.

"I'm stuffed. You're one hell of a cook."

Once again, Sam and John started the climb, but this time on the way back, Sam would have the massive rack tied to his pack.

CHAPTER 25

Tuesday morning, Jake, Wyatt, and Jim waited outside for Dan. When Dan finally walked out of the lodge and over to the three men, Wyatt asked, "Did you sleep in, boss?"

"No, I got a call from T.J., I guess a couple of ATF agents are flying into Missoula late tonight."

Sarcastically, Jake said, "Well, better late than never."

"Yeah, I told T.J. to have them hold up in Missoula and that I'll get in touch with them when I get a chance. I'll probably have them head this way tomorrow morning."

"Sounds good. Pretty damn cold this morning," Jake said while rubbing his hands together.

Jim laughed, then said, "This time of year, we can get some pretty heavy snow in the high country. Even lower down in Blake."

Wyatt reached into his pack and swapped his ball cap for a knitted one. "You got to be kidding me."

Once again, Dan rode with Jim. Wyatt and Jake took the Yukon, and the four men left the lodge.

~ ~ ~

At the log home, Bishop sat at the kitchen table, drinking a cup of coffee with the two black bags of money on the floor beside him. Hank walked in and poured a cup, then noticed the bags. "Are we leaving?" he asked Bishop.

"Yeah, we're leaving late this afternoon."

Sitting down at the table, Hank said, "Finally, I'm going nuts just sitting around here." Bishop gave Hank a blank stare. "Get Troy and load up the money and weapons in the truck. Did you ever make sure it runs?"

"Of course, It purrs like a hot hooker."

Hank finished his coffee and entered the living room, where Troy was playing a video game. "Hey, Troy."

Troy was focused on the game with a headset on and never heard Hank. "Jesus Christ," Hank said to himself as he walked up behind Troy and slapped the headset off his head.

Startled, Troy said, "What the hell, asshole."

"We're leaving, dumbass, or do you want to stay behind and play frickin' games?"

"We're leaving now?" Troy asked.

Sarcastically, Hank said, "Yeah, first, we'll stop and have a nice breakfast somewhere in town." Hank shook his head and said," Just get the hell up and help me load everything in the truck."

~ ~ ~

Jim pulled his truck down the next road circled on the map. Again, it was a long driveway that once again crossed over a small one-lane bridge. Dan said, "It's crazy how far back some of these people have homes."

Jim said, "Some people like to be unplugged and off the grid."

At the end of the road, a huge two-story cabin with several outbuildings sat quietly in trees. When Wyatt saw the cabin, he said. "Well, if I was looking to hide out, this place would work."

Jake said, "Yeah, it looks like a pretty fancy place." Once again, Dan directed the search, and once again, nothing. Over and over again, it was the same story. By the time they made it to Blake and pulled into the convenience store parking lot, it was late afternoon. Jim told Wyatt and Jake that there was a small deli inside if they wanted something to eat.

Right away, Wyatt said. "Hell yeah, I could use something to eat."

"Hey Dan, do you want anything?" Jake asked.

"No, I'm good."

Then Jake and Wyatt entered the store, and Jim and Dan stayed outside. Dan took the map and laid it across the hood of the Yukon. Then, pointing at a few more places circled on the map, Dan told Jim, "I think we can cover these places, and then we'll call it a day. The ATF guys will be here tomorrow, and we can split up the rest of the search with them."

When Jake and Wyatt returned from the store, they had four freshly-made foot-long subs and four drinks. Jake said, "Here you go, guys. You both need to eat something.

It's been a long day. You haven't eaten anything since breakfast."

"Thanks, I probably should eat," Dan said.

Jim said, "Thanks, guys. I guess I am hungry."

Wyatt looked at the map while cramming a big bite of a sandwich in his mouth and managed to ask Dan, "Well, where to next, boss?"

"Just a few more places south of town, and we'll call it a day. Like I was telling Jim, if we can get the ATF up here early tomorrow, then with their help, we can wrap this up."

After eating, the four men drove south toward Trapper Creek. After just half a mile, they came across the next driveway. It was a short drive to the home and produced the same results.

When they turned down the next driveway, it was overgrown with tall grass. It was easy to see that recently, someone had driven in and out several times, and the grass had been smashed down.

Dan told Jim to stop, and all four men exited their vehicles. Wyatt and Jake walked down the road a short distance and turned around. When Jake approached Dan, he said, "It looks like these tracks were made with a car or truck with some pretty wide tires."

"Yeah," said Wyatt, "like the tires on a Dodge Charger."

Dan felt excited that this could be where the fugitives were holed up. "Alright, guys, let's take this slow and easy. Once we have eyes on, we do this right. I don't want any surprises. Gear up, guys."

All four men put on their tactical gear and vests. Wyatt racked back the bolt on his FN SCAR and loaded a round into the chamber.

Jim's truck slowly eased down the driveway, when Dan spotted an old, run-down house. They stopped, exited the vehicles, and slowly moved forward on foot. The front door was open, and Jake pointed out tracks going into the old garage.

Dan took a position with Jim in front of the house and signaled for Jake to check out the garage. Wyatt eased his way to the side of the house. After Jake had cleared the garage and signaled all clear to Dan, he joined Wyatt on the side of the house. Then Dan gave the signal for Jake and Wyatt to make entry.

Meanwhile, Dan and Jim moved to the front. They could hear Jake and Wyatt yell, "Clear!" each time they entered a room. Then on comms, Dan heard Jake say, "It's all clear, Boss. It looks like they were here, though."

Dan entered the abandoned house. Scattered on the floor were beer cans and food wrappers.

"Over here, Dan," Jake said, signaling him into the kitchen. "Check it out. It looks like one of them got careless with a knife." Dan looked at blood stains on the floor and the table, then noticed that chunks of wood had been carved out of the top of the small table.

"He was here, Bishop, and the other two were here."

"Looks like your hunch was right again," Jake said.

"You and Wyatt take a sweep around outside. Jim and I will take a look around here. Maybe these assholes left something behind to give us a clue where they went."

After Jake and Wyatt had finished their sweep and had checked out the garage, they returned to the house. Jake said, "Nothing, Boss. You find anything?"

"No, nothing in here, either. It looks like they've been gone for a while. I'll call it in, and we'll keep searching."

When Jim returned to his truck, he grabbed a satellite phone, contacted the dispatch in Missoula, and then handed the phone to Dan.

"This is FBI Agent Dan Black. I need to talk to Captain Miller of the Missoula County Sheriff's Department ASAP.

"Yes, sir, right away. I'll transfer your call."

After a short pause, Captain Miller picked up. "Captain Miller."

"Captain, this is Dan Black. I'm with my team and Officer Jim Taylor from Sanders County. We're just one mile south of Blake. We just came across where the three fugitives have been holed up. I believe they may still be in the area. I need you to get your SWAT team geared up and headed this way."

"I understand, Agent Black, but I hope you realize you're a hundred-thirty miles away, so it will take some time for them to get there."

"I do, captain. Do you have any other officers that could respond quicker?"

"No, I don't. But I'll get with Sanders and Lincoln Counties and send all available officers to you."

"Thank you, captain. Me and my team are going to continue our search south of Blake. I know they are still holed up here somewhere."

"Alright, I'll get all available units heading your way. Be careful."

"Thank you, captain."

Dan handed the phone back to Jim and looked at Wyatt and Jake. "Guys, it'll be a while before we can get any backup. It's getting late, and it won't be long before dark. The way I see it, we could wait for backup or continue our search. What do you guys think?"

Without hesitation, Jake spoke up and said, "Boss, this is what we do. I say we find these assholes and not give them a chance to slip away in the dark."

"Wyatt, what about you?"

"I'm all in, Boss. Let's kick some doors in."

"Officer Taylor?"

"I agree with Jake and Wyatt. We can't wait. I'm with you."

"Okay, load up, and let's hit the next place."

Jim pulled his truck onto a paved driveway two miles down the road, followed by the Yukon. They drove a short way down the driveway under a huge log archway as they approached a large open steel gate. Dan saw the busted keypad. Jim stopped, and the four men got out and walked over to the gate.

"Well, looks like we found the place, boss," Wyatt said.

"Looks like it. Jim, get on the horn and see if you can get those highway patrol officers and game wardens headed this way. We'll hold here for a minute."

"Sure thing, Dan."

"Jake, Wyatt, you guys go up on foot and get eyes on. Comms up, guys."

Wyatt and Jake replied, "Roger, boss," and started through the timber.

Jim quietly called over to Dan. "They are on the way, the wardens are thirty miles south, and the two highway patrolmen are coming from the north and only thirty minutes away. They're coming in quiet, no sirens."

Dan nodded, then on comm said, "Jake, Wyatt, we've got backup on the way. Thirty minutes out. We're holding here."

"Roger that. We've got eyes on a huge log home, and just to the right is a big garage."

"Any sign of Bishop or the others?"

"Negative, but there is definitely someone here. There are lights on in the house. The place looks like a fortress, and all the trees around the place have been cleared out."

"Any cover?"

"No, very little. A few big trees here and there. It's not ideal." Jake replied.

"Can you see inside any of the windows?"

"Negative. There are a couple of curtains open in the front. Wyatt is moving to a position so he can see."

Suddenly the door to the garage door opened, and Troy Becker walked out toward the side door of the cabin.

Quickly, Wyatt said, "Dan, I've got eyes on Becker."

Troy stopped before entering the cabin and leaned against a wooden carving of a bear, then lit a cigarette.

Looking out toward Jake, Who was knelt down behind a tree, Troy caught a glimpse of Jake's shoulder.

"Jake, freeze. I think he spotted you," Wyatt said over the comm.

Troy stepped a few steps to his left, calmly put out the cigarette, then turned back and reentered the cabin.

"We're good, we're good," Wyatt proclaimed into his mic.

In the cabin, Troy hurried to where Jack and Hank were sitting. Then, anxiously, he said, "They found us. I spotted a cop behind a tree."

Jack and Hank jumped up. Hank slammed a sixty-round beta magazine into his fully automatic A.R. Jack grabbed his Scar.

Panicking, they moved over to two of the front windows. Jack turned to Troy. "Go to the back door. Make sure it's clear. Time to have some fun."

Jack peered through the window and spotted Jake. Immediately firing, a hail of bullets from the Scar shattering the glass window and ripped into the tree trunk. Wyatt returned fire, and Bishop took cover behind the thick log wall.

"Move it, Jake, move!" Wyatt yelled, again releasing a barrage of bullets from his F.N. SCAR and giving away his position. Hank opened fire, missing his target. Wyatt turned his weapon on Hank's window, emptying a full magazine, causing Hank to dive for the floor. Wyatt continued his relentless assault until Jake found better cover behind a stone wall.

Suddenly, Jim and Dan drove past Wyatt and Jake. Jim slammed on the brakes fifty yards from the front of the cabin, sliding the truck sideways. Wyatt and Jake laid down cover fire as Dan and Jim jumped out of the truck and took positions behind it.

Wyatt hollered, "Moving!" then fired his weapon into the window and took a position behind the next tree. Then Wyatt yelled, "Reloading!" Jake opened fire, then hollered, "Moving!" as he moved closer toward the side door of the cabin.

Dan hollered out, "Cease fire, cease fire!" After that, it was quiet in the cabin.

Again, Dan yelled out. "This is the FBI. Drop your weapons and come out with your hands on your heads." Dan knew it was a waste of breath and that this would only end one way.

In the cabin, Jack and Hank regrouped and reloaded their weapons. They had no intentions of ever giving up.

Troy yelled at Jack, "It's clear. We can make it to the truck."

A four-foot stone wall along a huge BBQ area ran from the cabin's back door almost to the garage's back door.

Troy went first, ducking behind the wall, then Jack and Hank followed. From where Wyatt and Jake were, they had no clear sight of the wall. Dan and Jim were still behind the truck; from there, they could see the BBQ area and the wall, but not the three fugitives tucked down behind it. Troy hesitated at the gap between the wall and the end of the garage.

Suddenly, Hank rose up and wildly fired a hail of bullets. Troy and Jack used the cover fire to dart across the opening and into the garage's back door. Jack yelled at Troy to get in the backseat.

Meanwhile, Hank lowered his weapon and ran toward the end of the garage. As soon as he cleared the wall, Dan fired his weapon, hitting Hank in the leg. Hank fell, but his momentum carried him behind the garage and out of Dan's sight. Hank struggled to his feet, barely making it to the truck and jumping in the front seat just before Jack slammed the truck in gear and crashed through the garage door. Hank fired his weapon out the window, causing Wyatt and Jake to dive behind cover. Troy opened fire out the sliding back window of the truck.

Jim and Dan fired their weapons, but the Ford Raptor flew down the driveway toward the highway. Wyatt and Jake hurried and jumped in the back of Jim's truck as Dan and Jim raced down the driveway.

Jack side-swiped against the Yukon on the narrow driveway, ripping off the side mirror. At the highway, Jack looked to the north and saw the flashing lights of the two highway patrol cars speeding toward them from Libby.

Jack turned south, and the Ford Raptor's supercharged V-eight roared to life.

Clutching his leg, Hank screamed out, "I'm shot!"

Dan's bullet had hit Hank in the thigh and missed the bone and the femoral artery. Still, blood covered his leg and hands as he tried to hold pressure on his wound. "Shit, I'm shot. I'm frickin' shot."

Troy was in a panic and screamed at Hank to shut up.

Jim slowed down just long enough for Jake and Wyatt to jump out and get into the Yukon. He then continued the chase. When Jim and Dan reached the highway, the two patrol cars raced by. Jim slammed on the gas and joined in behind the officers, followed by Wyatt and Jake.

The Ford Raptor was fast and had a head start. Dan could barely make out the truck a mile ahead, flying around the corners at over a hundred miles an hour.

The lead patrol car was catching up. Troy ducked down as Hank spun around with his A.R. with a full sixty-round magazine and fired at the patrol car. Hot brass filled the truck's cab, and Troy yelled when hot casing landed on his neck. Hank screamed as the rounds slammed into the windshield and engine of the patrol car. The highway patrolman swerved out of control and went off the road. The road's soft shoulder grabbed the tires, causing the patrol car to flip on its side and slide into the thick willows along the river. The second highway patrolman took up the chase but quickly backed off when a second round of bullets slammed into the front of his car.

At mile marker nineteen, Jack flew around a sharp corner. Immediately, Jack saw the flashing lights of the two game wardens that had set up a roadblock. Jack stepped harder on the gas pedal, and Hank yelled, "Crash through it!"

Suddenly, more flashing lights appeared on the horizon. Missoula and Sanders County Sheriffs were racing to the roadblock.

Jack slammed on the brakes and took a hard left, crashing over a sign that read '*Trapper Creek.*'

Jim and Dan had caught up in Jim's Ford F-150. So had Jake and Wyatt in the Yukon. But the Ford Raptor was built for the off-road and pulled away as it climbed up the uneven road. Hank clutched his bullet wound and moaned as the truck bounced over the rocky road. Rocks and gravel flew from the tires as Jack spun around the corners of the steep switchbacks.

Jack yelled out when he saw the road end at the Trapper Creek cabin. "Goddammit, it's a dead end."

Jack pulled the truck around Sam's Chevy and stopped on the side of the cabin. Then he jumped out with his weapon and went to the back of the cabin. Hank and Troy exited the truck with their weapons. Then Hank grabbed an ammo box full of thirty-round magazines and ran to the cabin door.

It was locked, and Hank screamed at Troy to kick it in.

Troy slammed his shoulder into the door, and the hasp with the lock loosened. This time Troy kicked at the door next to the lock, and it flew open. Hank slammed the door behind them, and both men smashed out the windows of the small cabin with their rifles.

Hank grabbed a t-shirt lying on Sam's bunk and tied it around his bleeding leg.

CHAPTER 26

S am and John were less than a mile away when they heard gunfire on the valley floor and stopped to listen.

John said, "Damn, sounds like somebody is burning up a lot of ammo."

"Boy, I guess. Almost sounds like full auto weapons."

When Sam and John reached the section of the trail with the downed trees, Sam stumbled and fell. The rack slapped against the rocks.

"Crap," Sam said in an anxious voice.

"You Okay, Sam?"

"I'm good. How's the rack?"

"Not a scratch, buddy."

Relieved, Sam said, "Good, That's all I need is to break a point off. This thing is definitely Pope and Young."

"I know, you're packing out a record book bull, buddy," John said." How about you let me pack it the rest of the way? I'll leave my pack here and come back for it."

"Alright, John, my knee is killing me. I'm having a hard time."

John took the lead down the trail. Sam followed just a short distance behind.

The two men were just two switchbacks from the end of the trail when Sam and John could hear trucks coming up Trapper Creek. John picked up the pace, and when John turned the last corner, he stopped just a few feet from the trail marker and looked over toward the cabin. He didn't see the Ford Raptor parked on the far side. Instead, looking back down the road, he could see the flashing lights of Jim Taylor's truck through the trees coming up the road, followed closely by a black SUV.

"What the hell, Sam? It looks like we have visitors," Sam hurried to catch up to John.

Worried, John frantically waved both arms above his head, trying to flag down Officer Taylor.

John never saw Jack Bishop coming out from around the cabin. Sam glanced toward the cabin just in time to see Bishop raising a rifle and pointing it directly at John. Sam wasn't more than five yards behind John when he screamed, "John! Watch out!"

Sam rushed toward John, quickly pushing him to the ground and out of the way just as Jack Bishop pulled the trigger. Two thirty-caliber bullets ripped into Sam's back, then exited his chest. Sam dropped facedown onto the ground.

John screamed out, "Sam! Sam!"

Jack Bishop had just fired two fatal shots into Sam Conner's back.

John scrambled to remove his pack, then quickly crawled over to Sam, lying motionless on the blood-covered ground. John rolled Sam onto his back and placed one hand under his head. With the other, he held Sam's hand, squeezing as hard as he could.

"Sam, don't die, don't die on me, buddy."

Finally, Sam opened his eyes and, with his last breath, said, "It's okay, John. Everything's okay."

Seeing what happened, Jim Taylor slammed on his brakes, and he and Dan jumped out of the truck, firing their weapons toward the cabin. Jack Bishop took cover behind the cabin, as Hank and Troy released a barrage of automatic gunfire from inside, riddling the truck and SUV with bullet holes.

Returning fire, Dan and Jim took cover behind the back of the truck. Jim motioned Dan into the timber to circle around. Wyatt and Jake had caught up and promptly joined the firefight. Even with their AR-15s, Dan and Jim were being outgunned by their enemies' heavy automatic weapons. At least until Wyatt opened fire with his F.N. Scar, sending a barrage of bullets into the cabin. Jake quickly moved into position for a better line of fire.

Just as Dan moved into the timber and took cover behind a large tree, Jim caught a glimpse of Hank Barnes through one of the cabin's small windows, taking aim at Dan. Jim fired a single round, and the bullet from Jim's rifle struck Hank Barnes in the head, killing him instantly. Hank dropped onto the floor of the cabin.

Over a loudspeaker, Wyatt called out. "Drop your weapons. It's over! You have no place to go!"

Troy sat bleeding in the corner of the cabin, with his rifle on the floor next to him. He had been hit in the shoulder. He was clutching his hand over his wound. He yelled, "I'm coming out. Don't shoot." When Troy came through the door onto the small porch, he dropped to his knees and held one hand in the air. The other was still covering his wound. Jim hollered, "Where's Bishop? Where's Hank?"

"Hank's dead; Jack is gone."

Still holding Sam's hand, John looked up towards the cabin. Behind it, he spotted Jack scrambling up through the timber out of sight of Jim and the agents. Overcome by rage and grief, John ran back up the trail, trying to catch up to Jack and cut him off.

After rounding the corner of the third switchback, he saw Jack sliding down some rocks onto the trail. John drew his 44-magnum from his holster just as Jack turned toward him and went to raise his rifle. John fired one shot. The three-hundred-and-five-grain bear round slammed into Jack's chest, and he dropped.

John slowly walked toward the man who had just killed his best friend, his 44-magnum trained on Bishop's chest. Looking down into Jack Bishop's cold dark eyes, John said nothing. Bishop was still alive and spitting blood from his mouth, still trying to reach over to his rifle on the ground. John slowly pulled the hammer back on the big handgun. Jack was looking straight into John's eyes when John pulled the trigger. The 44-magnum roared as the heavy slug smashed into Jack's forehead.

Feeling numb, John turned away and slowly walked back down the trail. Having heard the two shots, Jim Taylor was hurrying up the trail when he saw John walking with his head down, still holding his handgun in his right hand. Jim stopped as John walked past him. "Are you okay, John? Where's Bishop?"

John just kept walking and said, "It's over."

~ ~ ~

The following spring, John returned to Trapper Creek and drove up the rugged switchbacks to the Trapper Creek cabin. Beth sat quietly in the passenger seat.

As she gazed ahead, she told John, "I bet Sam loved being up here."

"He sure did. He gave me crap about how my truck wouldn't make it here."

She smiled. "That's my Sam."

John and Beth stared at the trail marker when they approached the cabin. Then, in a quiet, shaken voice, Beth asked, "Is that the place, John?" John reached over and touched her shaking hand.

"Yes, ma'am, it is." Tears rolled down Beth's face as she tried to calm herself.

When they reached the cabin, John walked to the passenger door and helped Beth out of his truck. Then he reached into the back seat, taking a square cardboard box from the cab, and handed it to Beth. Then, getting into the bed of his truck, he pulled out a heavy ax and a steel post.

Beth and John walked away from the cabin toward the trail marker. Just a few steps from the marker, John looked down at the ground.

"It was right here where Sam died, Mrs. Conner." Beth reached out and took John's hand.

"Oh my god, John, I miss him so much."

"I know, Beth. I do too."

Beth watched as John took the ax and drove the post deep into the ground. When he was finished, Beth handed him the cardboard box. Opening it, he slid out a bronze plaque, then attached it to the post. Engraved into the plaque were the words: 'In Memory of Sam Conner, My Best Friend.'

Four years have now passed since Sam was killed at Trapper Creek. John still works the graveyard shift at the Baylor mill and manages his small farm at home.

In his house, he sits quietly in his living room, clutching his hands together, in front of the fireplace. On the wall, John stares at a picture of him and Sam kneeling behind the giant, seven-point bull elk. Sam's bow lies across the chest of the enormous bull. Sam has one hand on the wide rack and the other on John's shoulder. Above the picture is the shoulder mount of the massive bull.

Below, a framed Pope and Young certificate, forever securing Sam's bull in the record books, sits on the mantel of the fireplace.

When John's young son walked over to his dad and asked, "Are you okay, Daddy?" John wiped his eyes.

Looking at his son, he said, "Everything is fine, Sam."

"Let's go for that drive I promised you."

In the driveway sits an old Jeep. In the back window, there's a sticker that says: 'The Money Pit.'

The End!

ABOUT THE AUTHOR

As an avid bow hunter, fly fisherman, and outdoorsman, the author often reflects on his years of adventures with his father. His passion for the outdoors has taken him from the low-lying hardwood forest of the south and the warm waters of the Gulf of Mexico to Montana's rugged, majestic mountains.

However, he is also inspired by his love for writing when he is not exploring the outdoors or spending time with family.